Dedicated to my beautiful wife, Julie … my inspiration

Contents

PROLOGUE

ー⌒ー

awn was breaking as fifteen-year-old Antonio Vasquez gently nudged awake his seven-year-old sister, Isabella, who was sleeping beside him. They had spent the night in the bushes on the Mexican side of the Rio Grande river, near the border crossing bridge linking Ciudad Juarez with El Paso, Texas. They had travelled for nearly a month and sixteen hundred miles from their home in San Pedro Sula, Honduras – one of the world's deadliest cities - and today would seek asylum from the U.S. Customs and Border Patrol agents at the U.S.-Mexico border.

As he rolled up their tattered blankets and brushed the leaves and grass out of his sister's matted black hair, Antonio prayed that their request for asylum in the U.S. would be granted so that he and Isabella could travel to their aunt's home near Houston and begin their lives anew.

As he looked at his sister, Antonio recalled what a happy, bright-eyed child she once was. He marveled how someone at age seven could actually look old. The light was now gone from her eyes. She had witnessed too much deadly violence.

Their father had recently been murdered by the vicious Mara Salvatrucha gang (MS-13) and, shortly after, their mother had disappeared … taken by who he did not know.

Antonio refused to join the gang and had been marked for death. Isabella would then have no one and would surely be taken by human traffickers and made available for pedophile officials and tourists.

Other asylum-seekers they had met on the Mexican side told him of how U.S. Border Patrol officers were positioning themselves right on the U.S. side of the border line on the bridge and preventing those seeking asylum from even stepping across the line, telling them that their processing facilities had no more capacity that day and to come back at another time. This practice was a clear violation of U.S. and international law regarding asylum seekers.

Antonio also knew, from what he had been told, that if you could cross that line and step into the U.S. they had to let you stay and be processed.

"Come on, Isabella, it is time," he said to his sister. Antonio picked up the backpack that was barely holding together, along with the rolled-up blankets, took Isabella's hand and they climbed up the brushy hill to the border bridge.

Antonio and Isabella had been among hundreds of desperate migrants who rode atop *La Bestia* - the Train of Death – a network of Mexican freight trains that travel north from Arriaga, Chiapas at the southern border. As a deterrent to migrants riding on top of them, Mexico had ordered the trains to travel faster. This had not lowered the numbers of migrants, it had just increased the number of deaths and crippling injuries from people falling off.

Antonio had carried two lengths of rope which he used to

tie himself and Isabella to the top of the trains. Those who did not take this precaution would often fall asleep and be thrown off in the middle of the night when rounding a curve.

Their only food came from sympathetic Mexican locals who would gather at the train stops and offer free food, water and clothing. When the train would start back up they would have to run to avoid railroad security men and board the train while it was moving.

They had not eaten since the previous morning and their battered plastic water bottles were empty.

Soon they were on the sidewalk leading across the bridge. A family of five from Guatemala walked in front of them. Antonio's plan was for he and Isabella to wait behind this family as the CBP officers stopped them at the border line and, when the time was right, run around that family and across the line.

His plan worked, and soon he and Isabella were being led to the processing building. Once inside they were told to sit and wait and were given water.

After more than an hour they were shown into a small room and were interviewed in Spanish. Antonio was told they would have to be detained while their asylum request was being processed. When the interview was over, Antonio was told by a female officer that she was taking Isabella to get a bath and something to eat. She never returned.

Antonio was moved into a locked holding area with other juvenile boys, given a bologna sandwich, some water and what he was told was an immunization shot. Five hours later, the boys, and some girls, were loaded onto a 56-passenger bus operated by the Department of Homeland Security. No one would tell him where they were going or where Isabella was.

They were made to keep the bus window shades pulled down and there was a locking metal mesh gate separating them from the driver and exit door. The bus was soon on an interstate and as best as he could tell by observing the lengthening shadows of the highway signs through the windshield, they were traveling east. He couldn't stop thinking about Isabella. Where had they taken her? Was she safe? Would he ever see her again?

CHAPTER 1

⁓

Il was a surreal protest scene: a detention camp for juvenile immigrants just inside the Florida Everglades on an oppressively hot and humid summer night. Three dozen or so protesters with their signs were gathered on the gravel parking lot between a desolate two-lane road and the detention camp.

The protesters had heard that more immigrant children would be brought to the camp this night … many had been forcibly separated from their families after legally seeking asylum at the U.S./Mexico border. The media had been alerted by the organizers. One local TV news crew had shown up. Their camera lights were attracting swarms of mosquitoes, as well as exotic moths and flying beetles. The drone of high-pitched chirps from thousands of unseen tree frogs was so loud it almost made conversation difficult.

Twenty-four-year-old Diamond Herrera and her mother, Robin, came to the protest together. It was their first. Diamond – Di to her friends – had graduated with a degree in journalism from Florida IT College in nearby Ft. Lauderdale two years earlier. She had spent those two years working as a freelance journalist, writing and submitting articles to local and national publications, with the goal of eventually securing a staff writing position.

She had learned about the protest earlier that day through a Facebook post. She was strongly opposed to the government's new Zero Tolerance policy that was resulting in the separation of immigrant families who were seeking asylum at the U.S. southern border. She had not been aware that there was a detention facility for immigrant children almost in her back yard. She hoped that what she would witness and learn by being part of the demonstration could lead to a marketable story.

Di still lived with her parents at their home in Dania Beach, a city just south of Fort Lauderdale. Robin felt the same way Di did about the immigrant family separations and child incarcerations. When Di told her about her plans for that night, Robin insisted on going with her.

Robin was just forty-four and she and Di were often mistaken for sisters. It was common for people to remark to Robin that they could see where Di's good looks came from.

At five-seven, with long black hair and striking green eyes, Di would be a natural as a TV reporter, but she loved writing and that was her sole focus. All her life, Di had been told that she got her eyes from her mother's Scottish side of the family and her hair from her father's Cuban side.

"Di, look at this place," said Robin, motioning toward the double row of twenty-foot high chain link fences topped with coils of razor wire that surrounded the facility. "It looks like a concentration camp."

"For children!" said Di, waving the insects away from her face and hair.

Rebecca Cross, the Director of Everglades Detention Center (EDC), and her chief of security, Captain Tony Lopez, watched the demonstrators from behind the front windows of the intake building.

"Look at those goddamn snowflakes," she said, almost to herself.

"Call six of your men up front, Captain. I don't want any of those people near the bus or the kids when they get here," Rebecca ordered.

The TV reporter, trying her best to ignore the bugs, held her microphone up to organizer, Reina Suarez, who explained, "This detention camp is owned and operated by the DCA Group, the Detention Corporation of America. They are a private, for-profit contractor that has been awarded tens of millions of dollars in recent federal contracts to incarcerate thousands of additional adult and child migrants and asylum-seekers who have been swept up in the government's Zero Tolerance immigration policy. As you know, many of these children have been forcibly separated from their mothers and fathers. The DCA Group is now reaping the rewards of their millions of dollars in contributions to anti-immigrant politicians."

Di, Robin and the other protesters spotted the headlights of the approaching charter bus about the same time that Lopez and six guards walked out of the building and toward the group. An array of blinding floodlights came on. The protesters shielded their eyes, raised their signs high and began chanting, "Reunite the children. Reunite the children."

The guards fanned out as Lopez announced through a bullhorn, "You are all trespassing on DCA private property. If you do not leave this property immediately you *will* be removed."

Robin reached for Di's hand saying, "It looks like those guards have riot sticks."

"I think what they have is the next generation," said Di. "I've read about them. They have a stun gun on the end."

As the guards advanced, the protesters backed up toward the two-lane road, still chanting. Since there were no police on scene to move them back, the local TV news crew kept shooting.

The bus pulled in behind the guards and up to the main entrance. The floodlights shut off. The bus door opened and the handcuffed children stepped out. First girls, then boys. They appeared to Di and Robin to range in age from four or five years to sixteen or so. The younger ones, especially, looked like they had been through hell. Each one had already made what anyone would have to admit was an epic journey lasting a month or more. Most of them looked like they were in shock. The smaller children had to jump from the high last step getting off the bus, causing most to fall to the ground.

The protesters now began chanting, *"Te queremos"* and *"estamos con ustedes"* ("we love you" and "we are with you").

Three of the guards made sure the children kept moving into the intake building. The other three approached the news crew. "Turn off that fucking camera and get out of here now," ordered one.

"We have the right," the reporter began before she was cut off by the guard.

"No, you don't," said the guard. "Not here."

The guards kept advancing on the crew as they backed up and climbed into their van and pulled away.

"Here they come again," said Di, as the three guards turned their attention back to the protesters.

The protesters continued chanting to the children in Spanish as the guards herded them toward their vehicles parked on the sides of the road.

Di and Robin loaded their signs into the back seat of Di's red Prius – a graduation gift from her parents – got in and headed down the dark road back to the interstate.

"I can't believe what we just saw," said Di. "A lot of these kids, especially the young ones, have been kidnapped from their parents by our government. There has to be more we can do beyond holding signs and chanting."

"I've heard that these detainment camps use volunteer translators to help communicate with the kids," said Robin. "You speak Spanish. You should volunteer, get inside and then write about what you witness."

"That's a good start, but I'm thinking bigger," said Di. "I'm thinking about when brave people took action against unacceptable human rights abuses. The resistance in Europe who risked their lives to hide and protect Jews and other minorities from being sent off to Nazi death camps. The underground railroad here in our country, where people risked their lives to help slaves escape. "

It warmed Robin's heart to see how much her daughter cared. "It would be good if someone *could* start a modern-day underground railroad to reunite detained migrant kids with their parents," she said. "But, since that isn't possible, you could do just as much good by learning more about what's going on there and writing about it … informing more Americans of this cruelty being done in their name. That's the way to bring about change today."

"Our courts have ruled that these separations and child incarcerations aren't even legal," said Di. "And the government didn't keep track of many of the asylum-seekers being separated, or where the family members were being sent."

"It looks like you have a story to write, my dear Diamond."

They were back in the lights and sprawl of southeast Florida now, almost back to Dania Beach.

After riding in silence for a few miles Di continued, "You noticed the construction equipment parked at the detention camp, right?"

"I did."

"That tells me that they're expanding it. There are more kids coming."

"I'm glad you asked me to go with you tonight, Di. That was an eye-opening experience. You *have* to write about it. If your dad or I can help in any way just let us know."

"Thanks, mom. I think I'll start by contacting the organizer who was there tonight, and tomorrow I'll call Everglades and volunteer to translate."

CHAPTER 2

The Everglades Detention Center site had been a camp for migrant sugar cane workers and their families for decades until harvesting became largely mechanized in the late eighties. The DCA Group had purchased the site four years ago, razed the old wood barracks and outbuildings, and constructed the current detention facility.

To the visitor – and the detainees – it gave the impression of part modern jail and part human kennel.

When the detention of immigrant children at the U.S. southern border had skyrocketed a couple of months earlier, the adults here had been relocated to other DCA detention facilities and quickly replaced by more than one hundred Hispanic children. Most of them were from the Central American countries of Guatemala, Honduras and El Salvador.

The arrival of this newest bus and the forty-eight Spanish-speaking children it carried did not find Rebecca Cross in a good mood.

She called Lopez into her office. "Shut the door, Captain," she ordered. "I want to know who leaked that the bus was arriving tonight? Ourselves and DHS were the only ones that knew."

Captain Lopez was a slightly overweight, mustachioed balding man in his early fifties. He had been working at

Everglades since it opened. When the Chief Administrator job opened up he felt strongly that he was the best candidate for the position, but DCA had transferred in Rebecca Cross instead.

Lopez looked her straight in the eye. "I have no idea. Who do you suspect?"

Rebecca walked behind her desk, still standing. "You can bet that no one at Homeland Security is coordinating with protestors. I say it was someone here."

She waited for a response, but Lopez said nothing.

"Who works here but is not a direct employee of DCA? she asked him.

"Construction?"

"No, they don't know our business. I'm thinking medical."

"You mean the doc?"

"Either him or that fruity nurse, Suarez."

All of the detention facilities operated by DCA and the other private contractors were required to have one doctor and one nurse on-site during the week and on-call on weekends. Doctor James Robbins and RN, Tomas Suarez, filled those roles at the Everglades facility.

"What do you plan to do?" asked Lopez.

Rebecca unwrapped a piece of hard candy. "I'm going to talk to them," she said, popping the candy into her mouth and loudly chewing it.

They could both hear some of the younger children crying through her closed door as they were led through the intake process.

"Goddamn it," she said, "I didn't sign on here to run a fucking day care center."

Actually, Lopez was thinking, you got this job because they could get away with paying you a lot less than a real chief administrator.

Prior to this job Rebecca had been an intake officer at a DCA women's facility in the Florida Panhandle for fifteen years. Even though she knew the procedures inside and out, Lopez figured her six-foot, 200-pound-plus imposing presence and her hard as nails attitude had a lot to do with her getting the job as well. She didn't like offenders, didn't like immigrants and, it seemed to him, didn't even like kids.

"Will there be anything else?" he asked.

"Yeah. Tell Robbins and Suarez I want to see them when they're done. And close the door behind you."

Lopez left, was buzzed through a locked door and headed down the brightly lit hall to the infirmary.

Dr. Robbins and Tomas were examining the final ten children who had arrived that night. A room-dividing curtain separated the girls, who Robbins examined, from the boys, who Tomas preferred. The children all had to strip naked for the exam.

Many of the children were openly crying or softly sobbing. The others stared straight ahead or looked down at the floor.

Lopez stuck his head in the door, "Hey Doc, the Chief wants to see you and Tomas when you're done here."

Robbins was examining a girl who appeared to be about seven on his white-paper-covered table. "What does she want? Why is she even still here at this hour?"

"I don't know. She has some questions."

Lopez didn't want to get more specific. He knew Rebecca was probably watching and listening to them on one of the more than twenty closed circuit TV's that monitored every inch of the facility.

A half-hour later Dr. Robbins, with Tomas at his side, knocked on Rebecca's office door.

"Come in."

Rebecca was now seated behind her desk. Her laptop was open in front of her. "Dr. Robbins, I no longer need to see you. If you are through for the night you can go. It's Nurse Suarez I have a few questions for. Close the door behind you please, doctor."

Tomas Suarez had recently moved from Puerto Rico to nearby Pembroke Pines. The twenty-five-year-old stood out in the facility with his man bun and one-inch black ear lobe expanders.

He knew that when the Chief started feigning politeness it was not a good sign. He reached to pull out one of the two chairs in front of Rebecca's desk.

"You can remain standing, Nurse Suarez," said Rebecca as she turned her laptop screen and pushed it toward him.

She had paused a local news video she had been watching. It showed the TV news reporter interviewing the demonstration organizer earlier that night in front of the facility. Across the bottom of the screen it identified her: *Protest Organizer, Reina Suarez.*

"Do you know this woman, Nurse Suarez?"

Tomas looked at the screen. He had no idea that his sister was one of tonight's protesters, much less that she had been leading it … AND was interviewed on TV.

He paused before he spoke. "She's my sister."

CHAPTER 3

⁓

Diamond Herrera had never met Reina Suarez before tonight. She decided to text Reina, whose number was included on the information sheet that was handed out to each protestor.

"Ms. Suarez – I met you at tonight's protest. My name is Diamond Herrera. I am a journalist and would like to interview you about the separations, detentions and your work."

As Di lay on the bed she had known for as long as she could remember she began formulating her plan.

As she thought, she realized she was staring at the protest sign she had made that afternoon: "Stop Putting Children in Cages," in black lettering on white foamcore board.

Her text notification hummed. It was Reina.

"Thank you for attending, Ms. Herrera. I can meet with you tomorrow. Call me."

Di had only sold two stories in the past month: one to *South Florida Pet Lover* and one to the *Broward County Examiner*. She was excited and confident that investigating and writing about the Everglades detention facility would result in an exclusive story.

Di quietly went out her bedroom's back door onto the screened-in lanai to call Reina. It was now well after midnight and she didn't want to wake her parents.

She settled into the thick turquoise cushions of a comfortable wicker armchair next to the pool. Since around 2000 nearly every home built in South Florida had a lanai: an in-ground pool close behind the home, set into a larger tiled area, all enclosed within an insect-proof screened cage attached to the house.

"Reina, this is Diamond Herrera. We just texted each other."

"Hi Diamond ..."

"Call me Di."

"Thank you for coming to the protest tonight, Di. These children need all the support we can provide."

"I know. My heart broke when I saw those poor kids coming off the bus and being herded into that place."

"That prison," interrupted Reina.

Di slid a cigarette from the pack that had been tucked away in her room since she had decided (again) to quit earlier in the week and lit it.

"I'm a freelance journalist, Reina. This situation touches me deeply. Not only do I want to be part of your demonstrations, I want to write about it, too. I would like to interview you and any of the other key people involved."

"I could meet with you tomorrow, Di – though I guess technically that would be later today."

"You name the time and place," said Di, stubbing out the cig after two drags and replacing it in the pack.

After agreeing on the particulars of their meeting Di asked if Reina knew anything about volunteer translating at the Everglades facility.

"I speak passable Spanish," Di told her. "And I need to get more information on the conditions inside."

"They do use volunteer translators when they question the children," said Reina. "I'll text you their main number and you can check it out."

They said goodbye and Di looked up into the moonless night sky and thought: tomorrow I interview an actual protest organizer and, hopefully, get inside the facility.

She needed to prepare.

CHAPTER 4

There were no supportive demonstrators at Everglades Detention Facility when Antonio Vasquez's bus arrived two weeks earlier. He had been taken eighteen hundred miles, from El Paso, Texas to Broward County, Florida. He had been handcuffed the whole way, except for the bathroom breaks at freeway rest stops.

The bus would pull into a rest stop about every two hundred miles. Each time, the bus would park in an open space between two black Suburbans with tinted windows. Once the bus pulled in, three men and one woman would get out of the vehicles. They all wore dark blue windbreakers with the word, "ICE" on the back. Antonio knew that *ice* meant *hielo* in Spanish. He wondered why these people, who were obviously guards or law enforcement, would have the word, *ICE*, on their jackets. He couldn't get over feeling sleepy, though, so he didn't think about it too much.

Meals consisted of pulling into a McDonalds and ordering forty-eight hamburgers and cokes for dinner, forty-eight egg McMuffins and orange juice for breakfast and forty-eight hamburgers and milk for lunch.

The bus drove straight through, for thirty-four hours, with each guard taking a six-hour driving shift.

All his thoughts were of Isabella. He was her only protector and they had taken her from him. All he knew was that she was not on this bus. Maybe when they get to where they are going someone will be able to tell him where she is.

One of the few words Antonio knew in English was 'welcome', and he had seen a sign about eight hours earlier that said Welcome to Florida. Could Florida be this big? He figured it was about four p.m. when they left El Paso and now it was late on the second night.

The bus left the interstate and was now traveling down a narrow, dark road. It soon pulled into a parking lot and stopped in front of a low, gray building with tall, barbed wire-topped fences extending out from it in both directions.

The bus door opened, one of the guards unlocked the metal gate and the kids up front started getting off. Once they were all inside the building and the door was locked behind them their handcuffs were removed and they were told to sit and wait.

Six boys and six girls at a time were led through another set of locked doors to what he later learned was the medical room.

When it was his turn in the medical room, he saw that it was divided, with the girls on one side and the boys on the other. They were told to remove all of their clothes and, one by one, told to bend over to be inspected. They were each given a shot, which they were told was *vacuna*, or vaccine.

The boys and girls were then led to separate shower areas where the guards made sure they all used soap to wash everywhere.

After the shower Antonio and the others in his group were shown boxes of donated clothes from which they had to pick out underwear, a shirt, pants, socks and shoes.

While they were picking out clothes, the boy who had been sitting next to Antonio on the bus grabbed a Star Wars tee shirt away from a younger boy. The younger boy tried to grab it back and the older boy punched him in the face, knocking him down, and put on the shirt. There were two guards watching them but they did not intervene. They just laughed and said things to each other in English that Antonio did not understand.

Once they had gotten dressed, they were led down a hall and through another locked door into a large indoor area with concrete floors and two large chain link fence enclosures … one holding boys and the other holding girls.

Antonio and the other boys in his group were put into the boys' enclosure. Their group was the last of the night.

The enclosure had benches bolted into the concrete around the perimeter and thin blue mats in rows on the floor, each with its own silver foil space blanket. Most of the mats were already occupied by the time Antonio was led in so he had to take one in the middle.

About a half hour later guards came with plastic trays with forty-eight bologna sandwiches on one and forty-eight six-ounce cartons of warm milk on the other. They unlocked the chain link door, pushed the trays in on the floor and said, "One per person. *Uno por persona.*"

The boys hadn't been fed since lunch and all rushed to the trays. As he picked up his portion, Antonio noticed that the boy who had taken the Star Wars shirt had taken two sandwiches and two milks for himself, which meant that one boy would not eat.

The boy's name was Adalberto. On the bus he had told Antonio he was from San Salvador, El Salvador. They were both fifteen. Antonio judged from the boy's neck tattoos that he was in one gang or another.

Antonio, at five-eight, was tall for a Honduran teen. Adalberto stood maybe five-two. Adalberto was about to walk past Antonio with his two sandwiches and milks when Antonio blocked his way.

"Put back the extra sandwich and milk," he said. "There's only one for each."

"Who appointed you jefe, Honduras boy?" said Adalberto.

The other boys stopped where they were and watched.

Antonio replied, "Jefe says put it back." Adalberto didn't move. Another older boy repeated what Antonio had said, "Jefe says put it back." Then another boy repeated the phrase, "Jefe says put it back." Soon, all the boys picked up on it and joined in, "Jefe says put it back. Jefe says put it back," they all chanted.

Adalberto looked around, assessed his situation, walked back to the trays on the floor and dropped the extra sandwich and milk.

Antonio went back to his mat and sat down with his food. He hadn't been able to protect Isabella, but maybe he could protect other little ones here. He would have to keep an eye on Adalberto he thought as he ate.

CHAPTER 5

D i phoned the Everglades facility first thing in the morning and was given a 10:00 a.m. appointment to interview as a volunteer translator. She texted the news to Reina and they pushed their meeting back to 3:00. Reina asked her to write down as many of the children's names as she could.

She decided her journalist look could double as a translator look as she tied her long black hair up into a simple chignon and put on her black-framed glasses which, since they had very little correction, were more for effect than for vision enhancement.

She arrived at Everglades, was buzzed in after clearing security and was told that Chief Rebecca Cross would see her shortly.

A few minutes later a guard showed her into Rebecca's office.

Rebecca stood up, came around from behind her desk and extended her hand. "I'm Rebecca Cross. I'm the Chief Administrator of Everglades."

"I'm Diamond Herrera. Very pleased to meet you." Di thought that this large woman looked every bit the part of a hard-nosed prison administrator.

"Please sit down," said Rebecca, motioning to a straight-back chair in front of her desk.

As they spoke, Tony Lopez was in a nearby office running a background check on Di.

"Entonces, ¿qué hace que quieras ser un traductor voluntario?" asked Rebecca.

Excellent time management, thought Di. She's asking me why I want to be a volunteer translator at the same time she's testing my Spanish. Actually, Cross had looked up this phrase on a Spanish translating site and had it written down in front of her.

"Lo veo como una forma de servir a mi país," ("I see it as a way to serve my country"), said Di.

Just then Rebecca's desk phone rang. She could see it was Lopez.

"Excuse me just a moment. I have to take this," she said to Di, and picked up the phone.

"Yes, Captain?"

"She's a journalist."

"I see. Thank you."

Rebecca hung up the phone and looked down at Di's application. "Diamond Herrera," she said without looking up. "Your name seems familiar. I believe I recall seeing your name as the reporter on a newspaper or magazine article I recently read. You have a memorable name."

"As a matter of fact, I am a freelance journalist ... really just starting out. I'm flattered, though. I didn't realize I had achieved name recognition. I specialize in stories about pets,

SEPARATED AT THE BORDER

hobbies, parks, society, those kinds of things." She knew she was suddenly in a bind and wanted to sound as non-threatening as possible.

"Do you read *South Florida Pet Lover*, by chance?" Di continued. "I have an article in the current issue on the rehabilitation and training of problem rescue dogs."

Rebecca looked up with a cold smile. "That must have been it."

The last thing Chief Cross wanted was to have someone from the fake media snooping around inside her domain. On the other hand, this was just an unemployed kid writing pet stories ... and she badly needed a translator to start getting information from these kids.

"Can you start today?" asked Rebecca.

Di wasn't expecting to be asked to start right away. "Sure. I guess. I have an appointment at three so I can't stay past two."

"That will be a good start," said Rebecca.

She slid a large stack of papers across her desk.

"These are the forms we need filled out in English for each child." She pushed a button on her desk intercom: "Mr. Cobb, I need you to escort our translator to the interview room."

She looked at Di again. "The interviewing rules are, no conversing with the children beyond asking and, if necessary, clarifying their answers to the immigration questionnaire. No touching of the children is allowed. The interview room door is to remain open at all times. If a child becomes unruly or is nonresponsive call Mr. Cobb, he'll be right outside. You can leave your notebook with me. You won't be needing it. You can pick it up at the front desk on your way out, along with your phone."

Di's phone was taken when she was wanded through the airport-security-type entry. She was glad that it could only be opened by her speaking the password.

She gathered up the large stack of forms. "It's been a pleasure meeting you, Chief Cross."

Rebecca stood up. "You as well, Ms. Herrera. We appreciate your desire to help."

Di turned to follow Cobb. "One more thing," said Rebecca. "If a child asks you anything about their parents tell them you don't know. You are just here as a volunteer translator. As far as you know they will be reunited with their parents soon."

How was she supposed to answer? Yes, Ma'am? Aye, aye Chief?

She simply answered, "As you wish," thinking of the Princess Bride just before she tumbled down the steep, grassy slope.

Mr. Cobb looked like he was younger than her and weighed maybe three times as much. She followed him down a featureless hallway.

"Here's your room," said Cobb, pointing into a small, bare room with a metal desk in the center and two facing chairs. "I'll bring the first one in."

Di put the stack of forms on the desk and waited.

Cobb soon returned with a disheveled looking boy who

appeared to be about fifteen.

"Go in there and sit down," Cobb said to him.

Di could see he didn't understand.

"Entra, por favor. Siéntate y podemos hablar," Di said, motioning to the chair across from her.

The boy came in, looked back at Cobb who remained just outside the open door, and slowly sat down.

Looks like I'm going to have a minder, thought Di, as she placed a form in front of her. The boy hadn't looked up since he sat down.

"Mi nombre es Diamond Herrera. ¿Lo que es tuyo?" she asked him.

Silence. It almost seemed like the boy was drugged or something.

She asked him again in Spanish, *"What is your name?"*

"Antonio Vasquez," he finally replied.

"Very good, Antonio. I am here to ask you some questions so we can help get you back with your people. Where did you come to the U.S. from?

"Honduras."

"Who did you come to the U.S. with?"

Silence.

"Antonio, we need this information so we can help you. You won't be getting anyone in trouble."

"I came here with my little sister, Isabella."

"Where are your mother and father?"

"My father was murdered. My mother disappeared. She was kidnapped. I needed to leave Honduras and take Isabella with me."

"Do you know where Isabella is?"

"No."

And so it went for nearly four hours. Di interviewed more than a dozen children. One was only four years old. Many of the younger ones were quietly sobbing. Others seemed like they were in shock. All were confused. Lost.

CHAPTER 6

D i's heart was breaking as she drove back toward Fort Lauderdale for her meeting with Reina. She had just interviewed kidnapped children. Kidnapped by her own government. Di thought about her grandfather's stories about Cuba under Communism. The arrests of mothers and fathers suspected of anti-Castro sentiments. Children being taken and sent to re-education camps. Her grandfather and his family were fortunate. They escaped Cuba in the early sixties. The tears were coming now. She had to pull over.

Di had composed herself by the time she got to Starbucks. She spotted Reina at a window table and joined her. Reina was a well-dressed woman who appeared to be in her forties. Di could sense her intensity.

They reintroduced themselves. "So how was translating at the jail?" asked Reina.

"That was one of the hardest things I've ever done. I think some – if not all – of those kids are being drugged to keep them quiet and compliant."

"Did you get some names for me?" Reina wanted to know.

"I couldn't write any of them down. They took my notebook and phone and were watching me the whole time." Di could see that Reina was disappointed.

"I do remember one boy and his information, though. He was the first one I interviewed. His name is Antonio Vasquez. He is fifteen. He came from San Pedro Sula, Honduras with his seven-year-old sister, Isabella. CBP separated them at the El Paso border crossing about two weeks ago, after they requested asylum. He is desperate to reunite with his sister. They have an aunt in the Houston area who told them they could live with her while their asylum case was being processed."

"Well, that's a start, Di," said Reina. "One of our people has accessed the Customs and Border Patrol data base of detainee information. Once we get names and origins from the children we can work on identifying and locating their family members who accompanied them. Once we get that information our volunteer lawyers can petition the courts to reunite them. I'll ask him to try to find Isabella Vasquez."

"If your person can access the Customs and Border Patrol records why can't they access DCA's computers to get info on the children they have?" Di asked.

"Good question," said Reina. "DCA's computers are harder to access than the government's. We're still working on it."

Just then a young man entered, walked to their table and greeted Reina.

"Di, this is my brother, Tomas. Tomas, this is Diamond Herrera. She demonstrated with us last night."

As Tomas took a seat Di asked him, "didn't I see you at the Everglades detention center this morning?"

"You did. I wasn't there long, though. I was fired."

"What happened?" asked Reina.

Tomas told them that Chief Cross wanted to find out how Reina's people knew the time of the bus arrival. How Cross had watched the news coverage in her office and saw Reina's name as she was interviewed.

"Old Nurse Rached called me into her office after we finished processing the kids," said Tomas. "She showed me a screen shot on her laptop of your interview ... with your name on it big as day, and asked if I knew you. I knew she'd find out anyway so I told her. This morning I showed up and the captain told me I'd been fired."

"I'm so sorry, Tomas," said Reina. "This was my fault. I shouldn't have asked you to help."

"Don't worry about it, *hermana*. In this town I can get another nursing job tomorrow. Besides, that was one depressing place to work."

"Tomas," said Di, "I want to write an article about the Everglades facility. Are you open to being interviewed?"

"I'll spill my guts about that place if you can keep me anonymous."

"I'll ID my source as a current insider," said Di. "That should take suspicion off of you."

"That works for me. Where do you want to talk? It's too public here."

"I agree. Can you come to my place tomorrow morning? I live near here in Dania Beach. I'll write down the address for you."

CHAPTER 7

T he next morning Tomas showed up right at nine o'clock. Di's parents, John and Robin Herrera, worked full time so she had the house to herself.

Di had coffee ready and she and Tomas settled in on the lanai.

"Can you tell me more about your job at Everglades?" asked Di.

"I thought you were going to keep me anonymous."

"I am, but I have to start somewhere and your job is what you know best." Di noted that Tomas seemed nervous ... unlike yesterday. He kept fiddling with one of his ear lobe expanders.

"Dr. Robbins and I basically give the kids exams when they first arrive, and treat them if they have any health issues," Tomas said.

"Describe the exams," asked Di.

"We take blood and urine samples to check for disease and drug use. We check ears and throats ... heads for lice. They have to shower. The smaller kids we bathe. We toss what they were wearing and they pick new stuff from piles of donated clothes."

"So, obviously, each child has to get naked upon arrival. Both boys *and* girls," said Di.

"Yeah, but the area is divided, with boys on one side and girls on the other."

"Which side did you work on?"

"I examined the boys and Dr. Robbins examines the girls."

"How do the children typically react to this whole process?"

"I guess you could say they don't like it much," replied Tomas.

As they went on Di learned the current count of children (156), and that there were only 40 beds, the rest of the children sleeping on cots or on thin floor mats with just a foil space blanket for a cover.

The growing numbers of children had surpassed their existing housing space so a new, attached building had been hastily constructed. It was the size of a gymnasium, had a concrete floor and two large chain link fence enclosures had been installed inside with chain link tops and locking gates.

Each held about forty-eight children – boys in one, girls in the other. All sleeping on floor mats with foil blankets.

"Are the children being given drugs?" Di asked. "Yesterday some of the kids I interviewed seemed spaced out, lethargic."

"If a child is overly anxious or unruly they are given Ativan."

"What's that?"

"It's a benzodiazepine tranquilizer."

"Great," said Di as she took notes. "Tomas, I've read stories that abuse has been reported at some of these child detention facilities. Is there abuse going on at Everglades?"

Tomas paused. "Well, I've heard that some of the boys have gotten into the girls' sleeping area at night."

"Are any of the guards abusing kids?"

"DCA starts their guards out at barely above minimum wage with no benefits," answered Tomas. "That pretty much guarantees you're going to attract the bottom of the barrel. And it *is* human nature that those with power tend to pick on the weak."

"So, you're saying yes, there is abuse by the guards? Is it physical, sexual, psychological abuse?"

"I minded my own business," said Tomas. "But you couldn't avoid hearing things."

Di felt like screaming. She took a deep breath and continued, getting more details on the facility, its ongoing expansion, some background on Chief Cross and Captain Tony, as well as more information on the DCA Group.

Then she asked one final question, "How often did you see children leave the facility?"

"Ever since that judge out west ruled that the families had to be reunited there have been a few kids processed out every week."

Di sensed that Tomas wanted to say more. She waited before continuing. "Are there other ways that children left the facility?" It was a shot in the dark.

Again, Tomas hesitated. He looked down as he spoke. "There is an entrance at the far back of the facility that opens onto a narrow dirt road that looks like it just leads back into the swamp. I had heard a rumor that a couple of kids hanged themselves recently … one boy and one girl."

"A rumor?" said Di, "aren't official reports written when a child dies in custody?"

"You would think so," said Tomas. "But once these kids and their parents are separated, the record keeping becomes very sketchy, even non-existent in some cases."

Tomas wanted to tell Di more, but he was thinking back to Chief Cross warning to him not to talk to anyone about Everglades … or else.

"So, you're sure or not sure that two children recently killed themselves?" asked Di.

"I'm sure they did."

"And their bodies were disposed of in the swamp?"

"That seems the most likely, but I didn't witness it."

Di decided to take another shot in the dark. "I appreciate your honesty, Tomas. I'm sure this isn't easy to talk about. This is very important, though. What is the worst thing you know about Everglades?"

Tomas dropped his head even lower. "They're selling children."

"They're what?" Di almost shouted, then lowered her voice. "Tomas, that's not possible."

"You asked me what's the worst."

Di's mind was racing. "Why haven't you reported them to the police?"

"If I did I wouldn't live to testify."

"Who are they selling them to?"

"I don't know. Traffickers."

Di could tell he was serious … and scared.

"I've already said more than I should have," said Tomas. "Actually, I'm not sure of any of it. Forget what I said. I was just trying to get back at them for firing me." Tomas stood up. "I should go now, Di. Please forget what I said."

Di rose, too. "I can't forget it, Tomas. I have to figure out what to do. Please don't worry. I won't mention you to anyone."

They walked through the house to the front door.

"Don't try to take on DCA, Di. They're tied in with the government at every level. I don't think they would hesitate to take out anyone who threatened their operation."

"I know you're scared, Tomas. Hell, now I'm scared, too. Just try not to worry. I *will* protect you."

CHAPTER 8

ack in her room, the first person that Di thought of was Mr. Taylor. Jason Taylor was Di's favorite professor at Florida IT. He taught Newswriting and Reporting during her senior year.

Mr. Taylor often drew on his experience as an Army Ranger in the Iraq and Afghan wars as teaching examples in his class. He served for five years in the elite 75th Ranger Regiment.

Di had always thought he looked the part, too ... more like GI Joe than a professor. More than a few of his female students would find an excuse to walk by the school's workout facility after classes to catch a look at Mr. Taylor pumping iron or running on the treadmill.

Di looked up his cell number in an online faculty directory and texted him that she had come across what looked to be a major story but that pursuing it could possibly be dangerous. She asked if they could get together and talk. She needed his advice.

Taylor texted her back an hour later. Could she meet him in his office after his classes?

Di thanked him and replied that she would be there. She began researching human trafficking and quickly learned that there were more incidents of this vile business in South Florida than anywhere else in the U.S.

She also learned that human traffickers often begin by branding their victims with their unique neck tattoo. Young girls – and sometimes boys - are usually shot up with heroin or other street drugs so that they become addicted, beaten to ensure compliance and put into sex work. Other victims are sold into domestic servitude or manual labor. Toddlers and infants can be sold to black market adoption agencies.

They are told that there is no escape, no one wants them and no one is going to come rescue them.

Di quickly realized that these detained immigrant children are the perfect victims. They have been taken and separated by long distances from the family members with whom they came to the U.S. Many of them could disappear without a trace due to the lack of documentation done by the border agents at the time they were detained and separated.

All Everglades needed was corrupt, compliant management to make it a human traffickers dream.

Di hadn't been back to Florida IT since she graduated two years earlier. However, as she walked under the palm trees and across the grassy commons to Neuharth Hall and Mr. Taylor's office, her warm memories were tempered by the awful reason for her return.

The door to Mr. Taylor's office was open and Jason was seated at his desk with his head buried in papers when she arrived. Di paused before knocking. He had grown a well-

SEPARATED AT THE BORDER

trimmed beard since she saw him last and his sandy brown hair had the deliberately tousled look. Her memory of him was confirmed: he was possibly the most solidly-built man she had ever seen.

Jason looked up and saw Di standing in the doorway. "Diamond Herrera, come in. I thought you would be up in New York writing for the Times by now."

Di laughed, walked in and held out her hand. "I'm still waiting to hear back from them. Thank you for making time for me, Mr. Taylor. It's so good to see you again."

Jason rose to greet her. She had forgotten how tall he was.

"You're not my student anymore, Diamond. I'm Jason from now on."

"And I'm just Di," she replied.

He motioned for her to sit. "You said that you had come across a story that could be a problem for you to pursue. Tell me more."

"It's about the Everglades Detention Facility just west of here where nearly 200 immigrant children are being held," she told him. "It's owned and operated by the Detention Corporation of America. Have you heard of it?"

"It doesn't sound familiar. Tell me more."

Di told him about attending the protest there two nights before, meeting Reina, volunteer translating and, finally, interviewing Reina's brother, Tomas.

"You're right. That's one hell of a story," said Jason.

"And if I'm going to write about it I'll need more documentation than just Tomas's word for what's going on."

35

Jason waited for Di to continue.

"Before I came over here I Googled the service branch you were in, the 75th Ranger Regiment. I read that one of the things you guys specialize in is dangerous rescues."

"Among many other things," said Jason. "And only in foreign countries."

Di could see he was thinking.

"You didn't come here just for my expert journalism advice, did you?" asked Jason.

"I know I can't ask you to get involved," said Di. "I just didn't know where else to turn. I had to share this with someone and, I thought, who better than you. If I went to the Broward County Sheriff they'd probably tell me they have no jurisdiction over a federal detention facility," she continued. "Do you think the FBI would do anything if I contacted them?"

"Even if they did," said Jason, "an investigation would probably take a year or more."

"All I know is that those kids need someone's help … fast. It's like DCA answers to no one."

"I want to think about this," said Jason. He reached into a desk drawer, took out a black smart phone, stood and handed it to Di. "I was able to keep a few souvenirs from my Ranger days. This phone is for you. I have one myself. They can't be traced or monitored. Each has the other's number already in its memory."

Di looked at the phone. It had no logo or brand name on it. She put it in her purse and rose from her chair.

"I feel better just having talked to you Mr. ... Jason," she corrected herself.

"I'll get back to you, Di. You're right, something needs to be done."

CHAPTER 9

J ason Taylor sat in his office after Di left, thinking that she was right … this did sound like a major story *and* a dangerous one to pursue. He also wondered how he failed to notice how attractive Diamond Herrera was when she was in his class.

He was aware of how serious a problem human trafficking had become in South Florida. One of his good friends and a fellow Ranger, Tommy Ziker, owned a private investigation firm based in Boca Raton. Jason went online and learned that Tommy's firm had worked on cases involving runaway teens who had fallen into the hands of traffickers.

Jason and Tommy were both members of the Ranger extraction team in Iraq years earlier that had rescued Army Private Monica Moore in the dead of night from the fifth floor of a hospital held by Muqtada al-Sadr's Mehdi Army.

He could think of no one better than Tommy to consult with on this.

"Hey Bro," he texted Tommy, *"a situation has come up that I'd like to talk with you about. Meet for beers later?"*

Jason wasn't halfway through the paper he was grading when his phone buzzed. *"Great to hear from you, JT. How about Patio Joe's on North Dixie at six?"*

Unlike most South Floridians, Jason was a native. He grew up in Doral during the eighties and nineties ... before it had even been incorporated as a city. He was a star tight end for the Miami Springs High School football team and earned a scholarship to the University of Miami.

The attacks on Sept. 11, 2001 affected him deeply, though, and he left a promising academic and football career after just two years to enlist in the army and join the war on terror.

Jason so impressed his instructors and superiors at Fort Benning with his physical skills and dedication that he was invited to enroll in Ranger School. At the end he was one of the twenty percent of his class that completed this most rigorous of special forces training programs and was awarded the tan beret of an Army Ranger.

The Rangers' mission is to operate as an elite strike force, which includes hostage rescue, and Jason and Tommy fought side-by-side in many such missions in Iraq and Afghanistan.

Jason was reminiscing on these experiences as he pulled into Patio Joe's parking lot. As he walked in he spotted Tommy at a two-top table in a corner of the large patio area. Tommy waved him over and more than a few after-work patrons couldn't help but stare as these two massive men hugged and laid a few good-natured blows on each other in greeting.

"It's been too long, Tommy," said Jason. "It's great to see you."

Tommy looked sharp in a well-pressed white Cubano shirt and tan slacks, his black hair slicked straight back.

"Business must be good."

"Business is *too* good," said Tommy. "In fact, I've almost called *you* a few times to see if you wanted to come out of your ivory tower and moonlight on a case or two. And here you're calling me. What's up, brother?"

"I checked out your website and saw that one of your specialties is investigating human trafficking," said Jason. "That's why I wanted to see you."

"Go on," said Tommy.

"A former student of mine came to see me today with quite a story. It seems that somewhere around 160 immigrant children who were separated from their parents – boys *and* girls - are being held in a private, for-profit detention facility in the Glades just west of here. She was told by a former employee who just left there that they are selling some of these kids to traffickers … the ones that have virtually no documentation. Have you heard anything about this from your sources in that world?"

"I've heard something about there being more young Hispanic girls who don't speak English coming into their pipeline," said Tommy. "I haven't heard anything about where they're getting them, though. I mostly work with parents whose kid has run away and, often, it's the traffickers who have picked them up."

"I was also told that many of the kids are also being abused and drugged," said Jason. "Tommy, this is being done in the name of our country … in *our* name."

Back in their Ranger years Jason had felt that Tommy, though one of his best friends and a dedicated Ranger, was a bit of a showboat. He wasn't sure if Tommy would be as moved by the cruel injustice of what he had learned as he was.

"I see you're still JT the bleeding heart," said Tommy. He took a long pull on his Corona. "I'm glad you haven't changed."

"What would we have done if these had been American kids being held, abused and sold to traffickers over in the sandbox?" Jason asked.

"If we had been ordered to rescue them we would have done it," replied Tommy. "Big difference, though … it would have been legal … unlike what I think you're getting at. Plus, it doesn't sound like you've verified this story."

"Here's what I think," said Jason, leaning in and looking Tommy straight in the eye. "I think that if these stories turn out to be accurate, *someone* needs to rescue these kids."

Tommy leaned across the table as well and lowered his voice. This wasn't a conversation they wanted overheard by the after-work crowd seated around them. "Jason, you've lost your mind. What are you thinking? You're going to chopper in with a team, neutralize the entire staff and fly out one hundred sixty kids? To where? No matter how you try to do it, it won't work, you'll get caught and spend a lot of years behind bars. Get real, brother."

As he spoke, Tommy recognized the look on Jason's face. It was a look he had seen many times before in Iraq and Afghanistan as they were about to set off on a life or death mission. Jason's blue eyes became steely, as if there was a gathering storm behind them. His jaw set like he was about to deliver – or take – a blow.

"Listen Tommy," said Jason, his voice low and serious, "before the Rangers I was just a dumb kid who only cared about playing football, getting a degree and getting laid. Then 9/11 happened and all of a sudden I cared about something beyond myself. And I did something about it."

"I felt proud, I felt fortunate when I earned my way into the Rangers," Jason continued. "But after my five years were over I didn't come back home the same guy. Some came home changed by what they had physically lost. I was changed by what I had gained. *Rangers Lead the Way* became my motto, too."

Jason finished off his IPA, stood to go and faced Tommy. "If this shit is true I'm taking them down."

"Short of doing a nighttime jump, let me know if I can help," joked Tommy.

CHAPTER 10

Rebecca Cross was at her desk working on the job posting for a new nurse to replace Tomas Suarez when her phone rang. It was ten p.m.. As the head of the Everglades facility, Chief Cross could set her own hours. She was free to schedule her eight hours per day, five days a week any time of the day or night she wanted.

Her preferred shift was four p.m. to midnight Monday through Friday. The noisier kids usually had been either tranquilized, restrained or put in isolation by the time she got to work. She had come in early the day before solely to interview the translator. She swiveled away from her computer and picked up the phone.

"This is your hauling service," said the male voice on the other end. "Is our pick-up still on for twelve?"

"Yes," said Rebecca.

"How many?" asked the voice.

"Ten," said Rebecca. "Make sure you have it all this time, plus what you still owe me from last week."

"You'll get it," said the voice. "Back entrance again?"

"Yes, the same," said Rebecca. She hung up.

The voice on the other end belonged to Victor Valbuena, a second-generation Dominican-American and former MMA fighter who worked out at the same gym as Captain Tony Lopez.

Lopez had told him about all the immigrant kids streaming into Everglades since the Zero Tolerance program had begun. Valbuena belonged to the Dominican Kings gang ... the DK's. He knew that his uncle Rico, a DK captain, had acted as a middle man for human traffickers in the past. He suggested to Tony that perhaps he could help ease t heir overcrowding and provide a little cash to Tony and his boss at the same time.

The first sale of children had occurred the previous week just after midnight. Victor had given the Chief his order: eight of the best-looking girls eleven and up along with a couple of older boys who looked like they could handle hard, physical labor. He would have liked more but he could only cram ten kids into the back of his uncle's Econoline van.

The selected children had been told that their parents or family guardian had been located and they would be leaving that night to be reunited with them. Rebecca directed that those children be given extra Ativan in their evening meal to ensure that they would be manageable for Valbuena and his helper.

All had gone smoothly that first night except that Valbuena had only brought two thousand dollars ... not the three hundred per head that had been agreed upon.

Jason received Di's text on the black phone as he was driving home from meeting with Tommy. She wanted to know what was their next move.

Jason pulled over to reply, *"Planning on doing recon on facility tonite."*

Di replied immediately. *"I'm going with. Where can we meet?"*

Jason knew it would be no use to tell her she couldn't come along. This was Di's story, plus she had already been to the facility twice. He told her to wear sneakers and dark clothing with long sleeves and pants and a dark cap. She texted her address and was told she would be picked up at ten-thirty.

Jason lived alone in a condo he owned in Cooper City, a suburb just west of Dania Beach. As he pulled his black Jeep Wrangler into his garage he was going through a mental checklist of what he wanted to bring. Since he had a Florida conceal carry permit he had his M-9 Beretta with him whenever he wasn't on school property. He still had his Ranger-issue boots. He had stopped at Bass Pro Shops on his way home and picked up lightweight TruTimber camo pants, a lightweight long sleeve camo shirt and a camo bucket hat. He rounded out his equipment with his Gerber paraframe folding knife and a black bandana.

His plan was to see if he could learn anything by conducting a few hours of nighttime observation of the facility. If Di did as he told her there should be no problems.

He texted Di one more time before he left telling her no perfume or makeup and to watch for him at ten-thirty … he didn't want to get out of the vehicle.

She was waiting outside when he pulled up. He could see she was dressed as he told her, right up to the black cap.

She opened the Jeep door, "Damn, Jason, you look scary. Are we going to storm the place?"

"Habits are hard to break," he said. "During Ranger school if you were ever observed during recon training there would be holy hell to pay."

"Were you ever observed?"

"Nope."

He continued, "Before we get there you'll need to turn off your phone and the one I gave you. Then take your phones and my phones, wrap them in that towel on the dashboard and put them in the glovebox. How far west on seventy-five?"

"Right where Alligator Alley starts you get off at the Andytown exit, go right, then another right. A few hundred yards down you turn left onto a road that's so narrow and dark you'd miss it if you didn't know it was there. That's the road that goes to the camp."

They were on I-75 now headed west. Jason took a couple of heavy rubber bands from his pocket and gave them to Di.

"Put these around your pants at the ankles. You don't want some unwelcome critter trying to get in there."

"Interesting," said Di. "I've never had an unwelcome critter try that route before."

Jason laughed. He was somewhat surprised at how relaxed she seemed.

"Have you ever hung out in the brush next to a swamp

for two or three hours in the middle of the night before?" he asked her.

He pulled another essential piece of equipment from the center console and handed it to her. "This is a mosquito head net. Put your hair up inside your hat and put this on before you get out."

"I can tell this is going to be a lot of fun," said Di.

She did as she was told with her hair, then put on the full-head net, the bottom of which draped over her shoulders, and looked at him. "I don't want you to try any funny stuff while we're in the brush." She couldn't hold it in and started laughing.

Jason had to laugh, too.

"I promise. Just remember, though, if what the nurse told you is true, we're talking about major criminal activity here. If the shift change happened at ten and if there's nothing else down that road we shouldn't encounter any other vehicles. I'm going to drive past the facility with the lights off and pull over as soon as there's a place we can hide the Jeep. We'll then take the best-hidden path of least resistance to a spot where we can settle in and observe the north side and the rear of the camp. Then we'll sit, watch and wait."

Victor Valbuena had recruited his nephew, Miguel, to accompany him. They left the run-down one-story four-plex where they lived in Little Santo Domingo in the Allapattah neighborhood of Miami at eleven pm.

Miguel, a skinny kid in hand-me-downs, was not much older than some of the children they would be picking up tonight.

They spoke in Spanish as Victor headed the Econoline toward Highway 27 and the Everglades Detention Facility.

"This is going to be a piece of cake," said Victor. *"When we get there, I'll pull around to the back of the place on a little dirt road. They'll have the kids waiting. I'll get out and make the payment. You help load them into the back."*

"I've got your back, uncle," said Miguel. *"If any of those kids get out of line I'll knock 'em out."*

"You won't have to knock anybody out," said Victor. *"They tranquilize these kids before we get there. They'll be like a bunch of sleepy lambs."*

"Then we deliver them to Miami, get paid and our night is over," Victor continued. *"This is good training for you."*

Miguel put his earbuds back in and they rode in silence the rest of the way.

Jason and Di had settled into a good vantage point in among some sawgrass and palmettos and under a live oak. Jason had pulled some of the soft Spanish moss off the tree for them to sit on and laid a folded blue plastic tarp on top of the moss. They were far enough away from water that he wasn't worried about gators.

Their position was about one hundred yards from the facility's north fence and one hundred seventy-five yards from the back entrance. The perimeter of the camp was well-lit so they could see it clearly. They were just a few feet off the rutted, sandy dirt road that led through the brush to the back entrance.

They had been there for a hot and uneventful forty-five minutes when Jason heard the faint sound of a vehicle from out on the road. Di heard it, too, and reached for his arm.

"If it comes this way we'll just sit and watch," said Jason. "They won't be able to see us even if they drive right by."

"I don't think anybody's out delivering Coca-Cola this time of night," whispered Di.

The vehicle sound was now clearly coming down the road they were on. The headlights were slowly bouncing in the dark and then the white Econoline passed them. After it was gone Jason reached in his pocket, pulled out the Jeep keys, handed them to Di and began whispering instructions.

"You take these," he said. "If those are traffickers picking up more kids - and they probably are – they're likely coming back this way. When they do I want you to take off your mosquito net and hat and let your hair down and walk out onto the road once they're about fifty yards away. Kind of weave and act disoriented, like you've been lost in the glades and have just wandered out."

"Acting disoriented shouldn't be hard after sitting here in the dark for nearly an hour," quipped Di.

Her self-assured words surprised her, given the situation. She realized that her confidence in Jason's abilities had her feeling almost invulnerable. Get a grip, she thought. Jason's counting on you ... we're a team.

"Position yourself just to the left of middle on the road, facing the van," he went on. "I want the driver looking to his right … at you … away from where I'll be approaching him from. I saw the passenger when they went by and he's just a kid. I expect the driver will be more formidable."

Di was listening intently to every word.

"We want the van to stop for you with the driver's door about five yards past my position. Look straight at the van and hold up your right hand. Remember to make all your movements slowly. Once the van stops stay where you are. We want the driver to get out. When he exits the van, I'll neutralize him and then gain control of the passenger."

Di could feel her pulse quickening.

Captain Tony was waiting at the back entrance for the van's arrival. The children who were to be sent with Victor were sitting on the hallway floor. Tony alerted Chief Cross by walkie-talkie when he saw the van's headlights approaching.

Victor pulled up and turned the van around so it was pointing back toward the way they entered. He walked over to Rebecca to make payment while Miguel jumped out and opened the van's rear doors.

"I think your people will be very happy with this batch," said Rebecca as Victor handed her a wad of bills. "You won't mind if I count it this time."

"It's all there," said Victor.

Rebecca finished counting and turned to Tony. "We're good, captain. Load them up."

"*Come on, children,*" said Tony in Spanish. "*You will soon be with your parents.*"

Jason and Di could clearly see about ten children exit the rear of the facility and climb into the rear of the van.

Jason continued with his instructions. "Once I have control of the driver and passenger you run as fast as you can back to the Jeep and drive back here. You'll find some zip tie restraints in the center console. I'll need five of them."

The van pulled away from the back door and was moving toward them. Di felt her confidence draining away. She took off her mosquito net and hat, shook out her hair and rubbed a little dirt on her face to complete the effect. The van was close enough now. She stood and staggered slowly out into the road, stood where Jason had instructed and slowly raised her right hand. The headlights blinded her so that she couldn't make out the driver and passenger. She backed up a bit and the van stopped right where Jason wanted.

"I need help," she said in a weak voice that Victor and Miguel probably couldn't even hear.

She could tell that the van had been shifted into park. Victor's door slowly opened and he stepped out, looking very suspiciously at Di.

Jason leapt up from behind him in an instant and cracked him hard over the head with his Beretta. Vincent began to turn around, Jason smashed the Beretta into the side of his face and he went down... out cold, blood streaming from both wounds.

He then pointed the gun at Miguel who looked frozen in shock and fear. "Keep your hands where I can see them and crawl over the seat and get out on this side."

He looked at Di who was still standing in the road with her hand still raised and her mouth slightly open.

"Okay, go," he said.

She turned and ran down the road to get the Jeep.

Miguel, his hands up, exited the driver's door, stepping over Victor's crumpled form.

"No hagas un sonido," Jason said to him.

His high school had more Spanish speakers than any school in the U.S. so he had picked up enough of the language to get by in most situations. Miguel obeyed him and kept quiet. Victor, still out, had begun moaning so Jason took off his oversized bandana with his free hand and stuffed it in the trafficker's mouth.

The van had been fitted with a piece of plywood behind the front seats so the kids in back were sitting in darkness. Jason said softly through the plywood to the children, *"Está bien, niños. Iremos dentro de un minuto."*

Di pulled up in the Jeep and got out with the zip restraints. Jason motioned to her to bring his phone, too.

He shoved the Beretta into his waistband, kept his eyes on Miguel and quickly zip-tied Victor's hands behind his back and then secured his ankles.

He then grabbed the slightly-stirring Victor by the back of his shirt collar, dragged him to the back of the van and sat him down in the dirt with his back against the rear bumper. He motioned for Miguel to join them, zip-tied his hands behind his back as well and told him to sit down with his back against the bumper. He zip-tied Miguel's ankles and positioned the two of them, one on each side of the license plate.

Jason motioned Di to the back of the van, took his phone from her and whispered, "Get the keys out of the ignition. Then unlock and open the back doors wide. Tell the kids that these are very bad men, but we are their friends. We will take them where they will be safe and then work on finding their families for them. Then tell them to stay right where they are, open the van doors wide, get out of the way and I'll snap a picture of Cheech and Chong here, along with their human cargo."

Di did as she was told. Jason said, "smile," and took the picture. He then took off his bucket hat and shoved as much of it as he could into Miguel's mouth, dragged he and Victor away from the bumper, took their cell phones, positioned them seated back-to-back in the middle of the road and used the fifth zip tie to secure them to each other through the restraints on their wrists.

Jason walked Di back to the Jeep. "You did great. You drive my vehicle and I'll drive the van," he said.

He then put his mouth to her ear and whispered, "We're going to my condo in Cooper City. Follow close behind me.

Try not to let anyone get between us … but if someone does, don't panic. When we get there, I'm going to pull into my garage."

He reached inside the Jeep for his garage opener. "You park right behind me in my driveway."

"You okay?" he asked.

"Yeah," said Di. "You are … wow! Yeah, let's go."

Jason retrieved their mosquito nets and Di's hat from the brush, gave a jaunty salute to Victor and Miguel, climbed into the van and headed home.

CHAPTER 11

J ason, Di and the children made it back to his condo
without incident. There was not enough room to open
the van's back doors with the garage door closed, so
Jason removed the plywood barrier and one-by-one they
climbed up front and out the passenger door.

Eight girls and two boys ages eleven to sixteen. They
blinked and rubbed their eyes after being in the dark for an
hour or so. Di greeted each one in Spanish and introduced
herself and Jason.

Jason led them all into his condo.

"Should I tell them everything?" Di asked him.

"You might as well. It looks like we're all in this together
now."

She told them all to find a place to sit and soon every seat
at the breakfast bar, dining table and living room was occupied by a silent immigrant child.

Jason gave a bottle of water to each of them as Di explained in Spanish that the men that picked them up were
actually kidnappers who were going to deliver them to other
bad people; that she and Jason were not going to turn them
over to ICE, but were going to try to find their parents or
other family members so they could reunite with them. She

told them she knew it would be hard but they would have to be very quiet while they were here so that no neighbors would hear them.

Jason was busy gathering up all the blankets and pillows he could find. Two or more of the girls could sleep in his guest bedroom, he had one couch and the rest would sleep on the floor.

After instructing the children, Di texted her mother that she would not be home that night but not to worry, she would explain later.

The children were doing as they were told, some whispering among themselves. Di suspected they were still under the influence of the tranquilizers.

After gathering the bedding Jason changed from the camo and boots into his shorts, t-shirt and sneakers. He stepped over kids on the floor and motioned for Di to join him in the kitchen.

"I have to get rid of the van," he said. "You're okay staying here with the kids?"

"Of course."

It was nearly two in the morning. Di was anxious for the next day to come so she could begin interviewing and identifying the children. She wondered if she and Jason were in trouble for what they had done. But how could you get in trouble for doing good?

"I'll take an Uber back here," said Jason. "Go ahead and get some sleep in my room. I'll be back as soon as I can and I'll sleep on the floor … don't worry, I've slept on worse."

Jason went out, moved the Jeep out of the way and left in the van. He was wearing the same cabretta leather golf gloves he wore earlier in the night. They were thin and soft, like a second skin, but provided exceptional non-slip gripping ability.

He knew he needed to avoid driving where there were surveillance cameras – a near impossibility in Broward County. He decided to head south on Hiatus Road. The neighborhoods he would pass would be single-family homes, not a lot of businesses. He wanted to leave the van on a residential side street within walking distance of an all-night gas station where the Uber would pick him up.

The problem with the communities he passed was that nearly all of them featured just one main entrance from the road he was on and each main entrance had a surveillance camera and, in many cases, a guard who checked visitor's ID's. He had to keep going south until he reached older areas.

After about four miles the neighborhoods opened up. He crossed Sheridan Street and spotted a dimly lit side street. He turned onto it, then quickly turned into a dark cul-de-sac and parked the van. He put their cell phones in the glove box and left the keys in the ignition. Maybe he would get lucky, he thought, and someone would steal it.

As he walked back north he shoved his gloves in his pocket and called Uber on his black phone for a pick-up at the Wawa Station at Hiatus and Sheridan. He felt a bit odd carrying the teddy bear he had found in the back of the van.

Di was laying in Jason's bed but she felt too wide awake to sleep. She reached for the black phone in her purse and texted Reina:

"Need help finding safe shelter for ten immigrant kids who were taken from traffickers tonite. All are safe now. Can your computer guy help find where their parents/families are?"

She doubted she would hear back until at least six or seven. She knew she should sleep but she couldn't help starting to write the story of this night in her mind. She laid back, closed her eyes and focused on breathing.

CHAPTER 12

The mosquitoes were eating the conjoined Victor and Miguel alive. They were especially attracted to the blood that had flowed from Victor's two head wounds. Fire ants had also found them. The first to arrive were painfully feasting on their victims' ankles. The next wave crawled up their legs, inflicting their fiery bites on every bit of exposed flesh.

They had by now spit out their gags and Miguel was screaming in pain and thrashing his legs as much as he could with the ankle restraints.

Victor was screaming, "Cross … Cross … Cross. Get out here you bitch!"

They tried to coordinate their movements so as to move their rear ends, inch-by-inch, down the dark sandy road back toward the facility.

One of the camp's guards had come out the back door for a smoke and immediately heard the screaming. He grabbed his walkie talkie. "Hopkins to Chief Cross, over. Hopkins to Chief Cross, over."

Rebecca was in her office and just about to leave for the night. She picked up her walkie talkie.

"Chief Cross. What is it, Hopkins?"

"Chief, I just came out back for a smoke and there's some people screaming bloody murder out in the dark down the dirt road. Sounds like two or three of 'em. It doesn't sound like they're moving, though. What do you want me to do? Over."

"Stay where you are. I'll be right there with Williams and Diaz."

Hopkins holstered his walkie talkie and yelled toward the voices, "Hold on, we'll be right there."

Soon Chief Cross, with guards Hopkins, Williams and Diaz, were walking down the sandy road, each with a flashlight.

What the hell is this, thought Rebecca, as they got closer but were still unable to see the source of the screams.

They walked around a slight bend and Rebecca couldn't believe what she saw in the beams of their four flashlights.

"Who's got a knife? Somebody cut those zip ties."

The three guards each pulled out a pocket knife and they set about cutting the restraints.

Miguel, who was wearing shorts, jumped to his feet and began madly rubbing his legs trying to kill and brush off the hundreds of ants as quickly as he could.

Victor was wearing long pants. He yanked off his shoes without untying them, tore off his pants and started doing the same as Miguel.

Suddenly he stopped, put his mouth to Rebecca's ear and said, "If you did this I'll kill you … very, very slowly."

He then went back to rubbing and brushing his legs. Fire

ants are so small and tenacious it was impossible to get them all off this way.

"We need a shower … now," he said. "You've got showers here, right?"

The three guards were not present at or aware of Victor's earlier back door pickup and so had no idea what to make of this. All three wondered why and what the bad-ass looking dude had whispered to the Chief.

Rebecca was acting as if this situation was as much a surprise to her as it was to them.

"Yes, we have showers you can use. Let's go. You can tell me what happened to you both afterwards. I'll look at your head then, too. It looks like you might need stitches."

"What the hell happened to you two?" asked Hopkins as they began walking back toward the camp.

"There will be time for questions after these men get showered and their bites and wounds tended to," said Rebecca.

They walked the rest of the way in silence.

Back inside the facility Rebecca told the three guards to go back to their regular duties and led the still-itching Victor and Miguel to the showers.

"What the hell happened?" whispered Rebecca to Victor as they walked.

"There was some dude and a bitch out there in the bushes," Victor told her. "Someone must have tipped them off about the pick-up. The woman was standing in the middle of the road. I had to stop and get out to get her to move. When

I did this guy comes up from behind and hits me on the head twice, knocks me out. Miguel told me he held his gun on him and made him get out. Then he put the plastic cuffs on us and they left with the van."

"I swear to you I knew nothing about this," Rebecca hissed. "This puts *me* in more jeopardy than it does you."

They stopped in front of the entrance to the showers.

"Go take your showers," she said. "When you're done come to my office. One of the guards will show you the way."

Rebecca started walking away.

"Make sure you have my money ready for me," said Victor. "I'm not paying you for no kids. *And* you're going to pay me for my van."

After they had showered a guard led the two to Rebecca's office.

"Close the door and sit down," said Rebecca. She took out all of the cash that Victor had given her earlier in the evening and slid it across her desk. "Here's the three thousand you gave me for tonight's kids plus the extra thousand to go toward your van. I'm only giving you that thousand because I feel bad for you. Since I had nothing to do with what happened I feel that is quite generous. You're the one that fell for their ruse, whoever they were."

Victor, staring at Rebecca, picked up the cash but said nothing. His instinct was to beat the hell out of her, steal a car from the parking lot and take off, but he knew better.

"Now I've got ten kids on the loose," she continued.

"And I've got no kids to bring to my people, no van and legs full of ant bites."

Victor and Miguel were still itching non-stop. The effects of fire ant bites linger for days, even weeks.

"So, it looks like we have a common problem that we're going to have to solve ourselves," said Rebecca. "Any ideas?"

"You do what you have to do and I'll do what I have to do," said Victor. "why don't you just call us a cab."

"No cab, no Uber," said Rebecca. "I don't want any record of you two being picked up here. I'm leaving now, I'll drive you wherever you're going."

Victor knew that he was overdue contacting Rico about this job but he no longer had his phone.

"Yeah, why not," said Victor.

CHAPTER 13

R eina Suarez always checked her text messages as soon as she woke up. As she did so this morning she was puzzled to see a text from a blocked number. She opened and read it and was a little surprised to see it was from Di Herrera, and more than a bit surprised after she read it.

Oh my God, she thought as she brushed her thick black hair out of her face. What has that girl been up to?

She immediately texted Di back, *"Yes. I want to help. Where can I meet you?"*

Di texted back Jason's address, telling her to write it down, delete the text, the children were with her and to come as soon as she could.

Jason had picked up milk and cereal while he was waiting for Uber at the Wawa. The kids were up now, too, and Di was serving them all breakfast. It was Friday and Jason had classes until eleven. Di told him again about Reina and that she was going to be there in a bit to help her get the necessary information from the children so they could begin the process of finding their family members in the U.S. They would also work on finding them safe places to stay. Jason found a blank notebook for her to use and left for school.

Reina arrived about thirty minutes later. The children were

being very well behaved. The fear that had been on their faces the night before was now gone and they were peppering Di with questions.

She told them she didn't have answers for them right now but the lady that just arrived knows a lot about how to help them and the two of them needed to talk. She introduced them to Reina, turned on a Spanish channel variety show on Jason's living room TV and the two of them huddled at the breakfast bar.

"How did this happen?" Reina was finally able to ask her.

"You're not going to believe this," said Di.

She told the story and when she was done Reina said, "You're right, that's incredible. I know people who can shelter these kids while we look for their families," Reina continued, "But you could be in real danger over this. You might want to find a safe, temporary location for yourself."

"Right now I need to get my car, my laptop, some other clothes and take a shower," said Di. "I'm going to call an Uber to take me to my parents where my car and my stuff is. Can you stay here and get the kids' information?"

"Of course," said Reina. "I can handle these niños. You go."

In addition to being an advocate for immigrants' rights, forty-six year-old Reina Suarez was an accomplished sculptor. She specialized in abstract sculpture in painted clay, inspired by South Florida nature. Her work could be found in galleries in Miami, Palm Beach and beyond. Reina was told at an early age that she would not be able to bear children. Her close friends believed this was why she had devoted herself so deeply to the cause of helping immigrant children. Her husband, Cyrus, an oil painter fifteen years her senior, had been taken by prostate cancer two years earlier. After Cy's death she devoted even more time to her cause, becoming a noted spokesperson and organizer.

Before beginning to question the children, Reina texted Father Pat Sullivan of Catholic Charities and Sue Ocasio of the Immigrant Protection Services Miami Chapter, seeking temporary safe shelter for the children.

She began her questioning with the older children, one at a time, at Jason's dining table. She had almost a Mr. Rogers-type ability to communicate with the kids in a way that calmed them and gave them hope.

She took down their names, ages, country and town of origin and the names and ages of family members they may have been separated from at the border or any relatives they were aware of who lived in the U.S.

Once she was done she typed the information into an email on her iPad and sent it to Rob Oakley, their volunteer IT expert, so he could work on finding the children's people, and to her contact at the ACLU for their records.

She had not been done long when Di returned.

"I texted the two best contacts I know of for housing the kids," Reina told Di. "I already heard back from one of them, Father Pat from Catholic Charities. He said he could shelter five of them. He's coming to pick them up around noon."

"Wow, that's great work," said Di, opening her laptop. "Jason's a super guy but I'm sure he's not crazy about using his home as a safe house for kids."

"Oh, and Rob, our IT guy, located Isabella Vasquez. She's being held in a detention facility outside San Antonio. I emailed her and Antonio's information to the ACLU for one of their attorneys to work on, along with the fact that they have an aunt in Houston. We need to get her name."

"Thank goodness you have someone like Rob," said Di. "I wish I had some way of letting Antonio know this."

"It looks like you want to get started on your story," said Reina. "I'll go hang out with the children."

Reina went into the living room and started playing a made-up name game with them to help her remember their names. The kids, it turned out, were more interested in peppering her with questions about America. Di set up her laptop at the end of the breakfast bar and began writing.

CHAPTER 14

———

Victor told Rebecca to go east on I-75 to the Hialeah exit. He then directed her to his Allapattah neighborhood.

Once they reached Allapattah, aka Little Santo Domingo, Rebecca felt like they had entered a third world country: five-and six-foot high iron fences with spiked tops surrounded nearly every home, church and school she saw; every window in every home and business was fitted with thick iron bars. For some reason, nearly all of the fences and bars she saw were painted white. With mostly one-story single-family homes, it looked like it had probably been an upscale neighborhood in some long-past decade.

They had made the trip in silence but Rebecca decided to speak before dropping them off.

"I have a pretty good idea who may have been involved in what happened tonight," she said. "We had a protest at the camp a couple of nights ago that was timed to happen when a load of new kids was arriving. The leader of it is a woman named Reina Suarez. Her younger brother, Tomas, worked for me as a nurse. I suspected he was the one who tipped off the protesters and I fired him the next morning."

"I also suspect a young woman who volunteered to do translating for us," she went on. "Her name is Diamond Herrera. She had to give us her address when she signed in. Once you get a phone, text me your number and I'll send it to you."

Victor directed her to pull over in front of an old one-story four-plex that had the same iron fence and barred windows as the other residences.

"I'll be in touch," he said, as he and Miguel got out.

Rebecca couldn't wait to get back to her upscale townhouse thirty miles north in Sunrise.

She didn't give any thought to the fact that she had probably just initiated a hit on two or more people.

Victor knew he was in big trouble. He lived in an end unit with his girlfriend, Maria, and her infant son, Eddie. His uncle and Miguel's father, Rico, lived in the unit next door.

Rico was in his mid-thirties and a captain in the Dominican Kings gang. He had already served five years in Florida prisons for assault and robbery. His short, curly hair was dyed yellow … it was too bright to be called blonde. His hair presented an odd contrast to his dark brown skin. The DK's historically made most of their money through drug and weapons sales and robberies but had recently expanded into human trafficking.

Victor had no desire to deal with Rico tonight and told Miguel to try not to wake him.

Victor had only slept for a few hours when he was awakened by a violent banging on his front door. The aching in his head and the itching of his legs brought back the memory of last night. He knew what awaited as he got up, went to the living room and opened the door.

As soon as he did Rico barged in and pushed him hard in the chest.

"Where are the kids?" he demanded, in Spanish. Rico shoved him again. *"Where is my van? How big of a fuck-up are you? Some guy and a girl take everything from the two of you? Yeah, you're some tough guy ... Mr. MMA fighter. You look more like somebody's bitch."*

Rico spit, contemptuously, on the worn carpet at Victor's feet. Miguel had obviously told Rico the story of the previous night.

"I got back all of the money," Victor replied. *"And I have a good idea who set it up. I'll get the kids and the van back for you and I'm going to kill whoever did this ... for me. No one does this to Victor Valbuena and gets away with it."*

"Big talk," replied Rico. *"You'd better get it all back, nephew ... or bring me ten grand to cover my losses."*

Rico turned and left, slamming the door behind him.

Victor went back to the bedroom. *"I need your phone,"* he said to Maria, pulling it out of her purse.

He retrieved Rebecca's number from his black pants on the floor and texted her, *"Send the names and addresses to this number."*

Rebecca awoke at her townhouse four hours later and texted Victor back with the names of Reina, Tomas and Di. She told him she would send him the addresses once she was back at work on Monday between four and five pm.

"Mierda," cursed Victor after he read it. *"You know how to look up addresses on this?"* he asked, holding the phone out to Maria who was still in bed.

"Maybe," answered Maria, a plump, heavily tattooed Latina in her early twenties, taking the phone.

"It's the three names in the text," Victor told her.

Maria propped herself up and began working on the phone. Victor got dressed and left the house to find two more DK's to join him on the recovery and retribution job he was planning.

CHAPTER 15

J ason was having a hard time concentrating on teaching his classes. He had acted instinctively the night before and had no regrets about rescuing the children from the two traffickers, but he now knew that doing so had most likely put Di in grave danger and probably her two friends as well.

He had already texted Tommy Ziker, attaching the photo he took of the van, it's license plate and the two zip-tied traffickers. He briefly told Tommy what happened and asked if he had a contact who could run the plate and look up the van's owner. He also asked if Tommy or any of his people could ID the guy with the bleeding head.

Tommy texted him back that the brother of one of his PI's works for the Broward County Sheriff and would run the plate for him. He also told Jason that the trafficker he asked about was wearing Dominican Kings gang colors, but he didn't have a name .... yet.

The more Tommy thought about Jason's situation the more worried he became. He decided to call him to share his concerns.

"Hey buddy," he said after Jason answered. "You really stepped in it this time. You know that these gang bangers are going to come after you and your friends, right?"

"That's what I've been thinking about all morning," Jason replied. "My former student I told you about who was with me last night, Diamond Herrera, did volunteer translating at the camp a couple of days ago. She probably had to give her address when she signed up. And her source is a nurse who just got fired from the camp, so they have his address."

"What are you doing with the kids?" asked Tommy.

"Catholic Charities is picking up five of them today. Di is friends with an immigrant rights activist who is working on placing the others in safe houses or church sanctuaries. They're also working with a computer guy and the ACLU on locating their parents or other family in the U.S."

"Hold on," said Tommy. "We got a hit already on the plate. The van belongs to a Ricardo Valbuena. Looks like his address is in Little Santo Domingo in Miami. We're looking up his sheet right now."

"Maybe I should just take this to the cops," said Jason.

"Not unless you want to add to your troubles," said Tommy. "They're going to say you should have called it in when you saw what was going on. Instead, they'll say, you stole the van, assaulted the driver and took the kids. You'll have to spend big to hire a good lawyer. Some of that shit could even stick."

"I wish you would have talked me out of this at Patio Joe's," said Jason.

"If I had known you were going to go Rambo I definitely would have," said Tommy. "What did you do with the van?"

"I left it on a residential cul-de-sac off Hiatus in Pembroke. I left the keys in it and their phones in the glove box."

"You done for the day?" asked Tommy.

"Yeah, I was just going to head home."

"Give me your address," said Tommy. "I'll meet you there with two of my guys. Then we're going to where you left the van … and let's hope it's still there. If it is, we're going to take it back to Mr. Valbuena."

"What?"

"The four of us will take him his van," continued Tommy. "We'll tell him this is the end of it. Whoever he sent on this job fucked up. The kids are gone. He's lucky he got his van back. We show him the photo you took and tell him that if any payback is attempted we turn it, and his name, over to the feds. Hopefully, that will be enough to take the heat off you and your friends."

"And if it's not?" asked Jason.

"Then we cross that bridge when we come to it."

Jason gave Tommy his address, said goodbye, gathered his weekend work and left for home.

Di, Reina and the five remaining children were still there when he arrived. Reina was still on her phone working her contacts. Jason took Di aside and told her about Tommy, Ricardo Valbuena and Tommy's plan.

"I wasn't too worried about myself," Di told him. "I gave them a made-up address when I filled out their form. You're right about Tomas and Reina, though. If those guys are part of a gang they could find them through Cross."

"And what if the address you gave is actually someone's home?" he asked her.

Jason's doorbell rang. It was Tommy and two of his undercover PI's, Hector Ramirez and Joe Costellano. Jason and Tommy introduced everyone before the four men stepped outside to finalize their plan.

Jason stepped back inside to tell Di they were going now. Before he could turn around to leave, Di threw her arms around his neck and hugged him tightly. Jason felt her firm breasts pressed against his chest, inhaled the feminine scent of her thick, dark hair and found himself returning her embrace.

"You be careful and come back to me safe, Jason," she whispered into his ear. "We still have a lot more catching up to do."

Even with the rugged good looks he had been blessed with, Jason always had trouble finding the right words to say in intimate situations with an attractive woman. Plus, Di's embrace and words had caught him completely off guard.

They stepped apart and he took her hands in his. "Don't worry, I'll be careful. Promise me you'll stay here until I get back. Hopefully, this won't take too long."

Jason could see Reina over Di's shoulder in the kitchen on her phone. She was smiling and giving Jason a thumbs up.

Back outside Jason joined the other three men in Tommy's black Escalade. They all were armed with concealed handguns.

Jason directed Tommy to Hiatus Rd. and they then drove south a few miles until they reached Redwood Ave. where they took a left and saw the van still sitting on the adjacent cul-de-sac.

Tommy pulled up alongside the van, just close enough to open the passenger door of the Escalade. He reached under his seat, pulled out a GPS tracking device and handed it to Hector.

Hector got out, laid down on his back, wriggled under the van and attached the GPS tracker.

As he was doing so Tommy explained to Jason, "After we get back you all are going to load the app for this tracker onto your phones. Then I'll program in the addresses and phone numbers of your people plus me and our guys into the GPS tracking app so that if this van gets within two miles of any of us an alert will go off on our phones. When it does and you click on the alert a map will come up tracking in real time where the van is going."

Hector got back in and Tommy continued to Jason, "I have Valbuena's address in my GPS," Tommy said to Jason. "There is no direct route from here to Allapattah and the traffic will probably be pretty heavy so try to stay with me. We need to pull up together."

"What's the plan when we get there?" asked Jason.

"We pull up together," repeated Tommy, who looked as sharp as he did at Patio Joe's. "You get out of the van, leave the keys in it, put their phones on the passenger seat and come get in the back seat of my vehicle on the driver's side. I want to avoid anyone inside recognizing you from last night, if possible. Then I want to sit there for a minute to see if any-one sees the van and comes out. If no one exits the residence I'll walk up to the front door and Hector and Joe will get out and stand watch."

Hector Ramirez and Joe Costellano were, as usual, dressed in their undercover mode, complete with full beards, black wrap-around shades and extensive arm tattoos. They defi-nitely looked like two guys who any sane person would think twice about confronting.

Jason was able to stay right behind Tommy all the way to Allapattah and they were soon in Little Santo Domingo – a neighborhood within a neighborhood – and pulling up to Ri-cardo's address.

Jason did as Tommy told him and got in the back seat next to Joe. They were there for just thirty seconds or so when a man came out of one of the front doors of the fourplex and stood on the step staring at them.

Tommy got out and walked to the iron fence.

"I'm looking for Ricardo Valbuena," he said to the man.

"That's my van," said the man.

"Then you must be Mr. Valbuena," replied Tommy. "We found your van parked where it shouldn't be, ran the plate, found your address and we're bringing it back to you."

"So, you're cops?" said Rico, walking toward him.

"No, not cops," said Tommy. "Just concerned citizens try-ing to do a good deed."

By this time Hector and Joe had gotten out and were standing behind and to either side of Tommy.

"The keys are in the van," said Tommy. "And we found two phones inside. They're on the passenger seat.

"I have a phone, too," continued Tommy. He already had his phone in his hand so he wouldn't have to reach in his pocket for it. He turned it on and Jason's photo from the night before appeared on the screen. He held it up between the bars as Rico walked closer to take a look.

"I assume since this is your van that you know these guys," said Tommy, looking straight at Rico.

Ricardo reached for the phone and Tommy pulled it back. Other residents of the fourplex had come out and were standing on their steps watching.

"I think you got a good enough look," said Tommy. "Listen, we both know that your guys fucked up last night. We're bringing your van back to you to let you know that this is the end of it. If any pay back is attempted, this photo goes straight to the FBI. Tell me you understand me."

"Yeah, I understand," Rico finally replied.

"Good. Then our work here is done," said Tommy, smiling. "You have a nice day."

Tommy and Hector got back in the front seat of the Escalade. Joe waited until they were in then backed into the back seat, never taking his eyes off Rico, and they drove off.

Victor and the two DK's he had recruited were among those standing on their steps watching the scene unfold. As the Suburban pulled away he walked quickly over to Rico.

"Uncle, you got your van back," he exclaimed.

Rico, with a dark look on his face, slapped Victor hard. Victor looked shocked.

"You didn't tell me they took your picture," growled Rico. "*With* Miguel … *and* the license plate. You're even more stupid than I thought you were."

CHAPTER 16

eina's phone calling had paid off. She found two safe houses whose owners had said they could take care of the remaining five children. Reina would drive them to the homes.

She was also receiving some tentative good news from Rob and the ACLU that they may have located a few parents and family members. The ACLU was receiving significant donations from concerned people in the U.S. and beyond that allowed them to pay for airfare for separated children, along with a volunteer guardian, to travel to reunite with their parent or other family member. Whenever possible, these volunteers were immigration attorneys who donated their time and expertise to do what they could to rectify these tragic situations.

Di had her story outlined - from the nighttime demonstration at Everglades all the way to the previous night's rescue. She was certain that this story would be of interest far beyond Florida. She needed to ask Jason if he had any editor contacts with appropriate publications.

On the drive back to the condo, Jason and Tommy discussed what should be their next move. They were in agreement that more of the children at Everglades were in danger of being sold to the traffickers ... not to mention the abuse and drugging that they were being subjected to while being held. They had no quick answers and decided they would each give the situation more thought and talk again the next day.

Tommy pulled into Jason's driveway and Jason asked if they all had time to come in for a beer. They did.

Inside, Jason retrieved five beers … Di was ready for one, too. Reina was gathering up the children. She had prepped them on what to say before they left:

"Gracias señor Jason. Gracias señorita Herrera," they said, almost in unison.

As soon as they were out the door, Di asked Jason, "So what happened? How did it go?"

Jason quickly told her the story and then Tommy took over to explain the GPS tracking app. Tommy had brought his laptop in and was entering their addresses while Jason and Di downloaded the app to their phones. Di gave Reina's address to Tommy. Jason sent them all last night's photo.

Tommy had overheard Di telling Jason about submitting the story for publication.

"Please leave any mention of me and my men out of your story," he asked Di.

"Of course," she replied. "Thank you so much for helping."

Tommy closed his laptop. He and his men had finished their beers. They stood and Jason walked with them to the front door.

"I can't thank you all enough," Jason said to them. "You always were better at strategy and planning," he said to Tommy.

"Well, I've got more experience," said Tommy. "I do this for a living now. You were always the better fighter, though."

Jason shook their hands, thanked Hector and Joe one more time and went back in his condo.

"I've had students come back to me before looking for advice, but you take the cake, Miss Herrera" Jason said, walking over to her.

"I'm sorry now that I did," said Di. "Look at all the trouble I've gotten you into."

Jason was wondering if Di had changed clothes while he was gone. She was wearing a tight, white tee shirt top with a deep V neckline and cut-off denim shorts. "She couldn't have been wearing that, I would have noticed," Jason thought.

"Another beer?" he asked her.

"Only if you're joining me," she said.

Jason grabbed two bottles from the fridge, turned and saw that Di was sitting on the couch in the living room. He handed her beer to her and sat down. Di immediately held up her bottle to toast.

"Here's to getting *all* of those kids out of there," she said, clinking her bottle to his.

"Here's to you getting your story published," said Jason.

Just then the GPS alert on Di's phone started buzzing.

◦◦◦

Victor was humiliated and pissed off by what Rico had done and said … in front of the other gang members and the women and children who had come out to watch. He was trying to decide how to react. He couldn't go after Rico. Just then Maria came out.

"Victor, some *puta* is calling you on my phone," she called to him.

Victor hurried over to her and took the phone. It was Rebecca Cross.

"Victor," she said. "I have the address of the bitch that volunteered for me. She has to be the same one who stopped your van. She can take us both down. Get something to write with."

Rebecca had googled "Diamond Herrera" and found her address on a freelance writers' website.

Victor hurried inside. "Okay, go."

Rebecca gave him the address of Di's parents' home.

"You have to take her out," Rebecca told him. "Then we have to find the son of a bitch that was with her, that fucked up you and your cousin. Maybe if we're lucky they'll both be there."

"Some men showed up at my house," Victor told her. "They brought the van back. They also had the picture the dude took of me and Miguel with the kids in the van."

"What picture?" Rebecca shouted into Victor's ear. "You didn't tell me about any picture."

Victor told her about the posed photo Jason took.

"Jesus Christ," she said. "How many men came to your house?"

"Four. They looked like cops but said they weren't," Victor answered.

"If they were cops we'd both have been brought in for questioning by now," she said. "Did you get their license number?"

"No," he said. "But my uncle might have. I'll ask him. Do you want it?"

"Yes, Victor, I want it," Rebecca said, like she was talking to a five-year-old. "Go check and call me back."

Victor hurried next door and knocked. Rico answered.

"Ah, my nephew, the genius. What can I do for you, nephew?"

"Uncle Rico, I got the address of the bitch that was helping that dude last night. Cross from Everglades got it. She wants to know if you got the license of the Escalade."

"So, you coming here means *you* didn't think to remember their plate. No one taught you how to think, did they, nephew?"

"I just need the license number, Uncle. I think Cross has a way to look up the owner."

Rico went inside, wrote down the license number, came back and gave it to Victor.

"I suppose Cross wants you to take care of this woman," said Rico.

"Don't we have to?" asked Victor.

"So, you take out the woman, then find her partner and take him out, then Cross gives you the owner of the Escalade so you have to take him out, too. What about the other two guys?"

"Maybe once we find the Escalade owner we make him take us to those other two guys and we finish all of them," said Victor.

"That sounds like a lot of work," said Rico. "How much is she paying you?"

"She didn't say she was paying me anything."

"So, you're going to go off and do all this killing for free," said Rico. "Mierda. Tell Cross you want a full load of kids for each one you do."

"That's a great idea, Uncle," said Victor. "A *great* idea."

"You taking those two?" asked Rico, looking over at the two DK's still waiting by Victor's front door.

"Yeah. They're good shots and I trust them."

"Good luck," said Rico and he went back inside.

Victor went out to the van and got his and Miguel's cell phones. He told Enano, one of the two DK's, to bring Miguel's phone to Rico while he called Rebecca on his.

"I have the license number," he said after Rebecca answered.

After he read it off to her he said, "You know, what we're talking about is dangerous work. I notice that you haven't volunteered to do anything."

"I'm not the one who fucked up, Victor," she said.

"Well, I'm not the one who caused them to know to be there. I'm just saying, my boys and I need to be paid for this."

"I don't have any money to pay you with," she said.

"It doesn't have to be money," Victor replied. "I want one full load of kids for each one we take care of."

"I can't safely deliver that many kids right now. I'll do one full load for every two you take care of."

"That'll work," said Victor. "I've got to go. I have business to take care of."

"Do you know where Dania Beach *is*?" asked Rebecca. "Do you have a GPS to find the address?"

"I have a GPS on my phone. I'll find it," said Victor.

John and Robin Herrera were both a youthful forty-four years old. Robin still wore her dark hair long, the way John liked it. Di was their only child. Both were CPA's and they had their own accounting business. They typically only worked a half day on Fridays and came home for lunch together on their lanai - weather permitting.

They had just sat down for their lunch when Robin's phone rang. It was Di.

"Hey, honey, how are you?" asked Robin.

"Mom, is dad with you?"

"Yes, we're just sitting down to lunch."

"Mom, you and dad need to leave the house right now. Leave your lunch and go right now."

"Di, what is it?"

"I'm doing a story about some very bad men ... gang members. They're coming after me and they have our address. Please, this is very serious. They're almost to the house. Go now!"

Robin had never heard Di this upset … and scared.

"John, Di says we have to leave the house right away. We're in danger. She's frantic."

John got up. "Let's go, then."

They had both parked inside their double garage. They left the food on the table. John grabbed the keys to his Highlander and they rushed out to the garage.

Victor had finally found the right street and he and his men pulled up just as John and Robin came into their garage and opened the garage door. Victor parked the van blocking the driveway, saw Robin and announced, "That's her."

Then John came into their view and Victor added, "There's the dude, too. Let's go."

The three gang members' handguns were fitted with homemade silencers. They rushed up toward the garage entrance, all firing at John and Robin. The two were hit multiple times and went down.

"Let's go," said Victor. They piled back into the van, made a u-turn and sped away.

Di and Jason were almost to the house. They turned onto Di's street just as the white van sped past them.

Di saw the van and screamed, "No!"

Jason pulled into the driveway, slammed on the brakes and they both jumped out and ran to John and Robin. Jason already had his phone out and was calling 911.

Di bent over her mother, who was bleeding from her left chest, while Jason tended to her father. Jason, like every Army Ranger, was given extensive medical training in the treatment of bullet wounds. Jason told Di to press the palm of her hand tightly over her mother's chest wound, so as to not let more air escape from her lung. Jason had taken off his belt and was making a tourniquet on John's leg wound. He had also been hit in his arm and side. He was still conscious.

Robin was close to being in shock from her collapsing lung. Another bullet had grazed the side of her head. They were both losing a lot of blood.

It seemed a lot longer to Di, but the first ambulance arrived within a few minutes. Neighbors had gathered on the street. The two EMT's split up, with one working on each victim. One told them that it looked like the bullet that hit Robin in the chest had gone through her left lung and that her head wound looked bad but wasn't life threatening.

The second ambulance arrived a minute later. The two EMT's in the garage yelled to them to bring both stretchers and a ventilator.

Di knelt over her dad. "You're going to make it, dad. Mom's gonna make it, too. I'm so sorry," she said.

The EMT's lifted John onto the flattened stretcher, then popped it up to rolling height. An IV had already been attached.

Di stood, grabbed Jason by the arm and spun him around. "This is your fault," she shouted. "Why did I even come to you. You had to be the hero. Jesus, God!"

Di turned and walked with her mother's stretcher as the EMT's rolled her to the second ambulance. "I'm their daughter," she said to them. "I'm going with you."

As that ambulance closed its doors and pulled out of the driveway two Broward County Sheriff's cars pulled up, followed close behind by an unmarked detective's car.

Jason was standing at the entrance to the garage. He had quite a bit of blood on him from tending to John's wounds. The cops got out, crouched behind their cars with their guns trained on him and told him to get down on the ground. Jason obeyed and laid face-down on the driveway. They approached him slowly and one of them handcuffed him behind his back while the others held their guns on him.

The plainclothes detective told them to get him on his feet.

"I'm Detective Lieutenant Bardo with the Broward County Sheriff. Who are you and what happened here?" the plainclothesman asked Jason.

"My name is Jason Taylor. I should tell you I have a handgun in a back holster under my shirt. My permit is in my wallet in my back pocket."

A sheriff's deputy removed Jason's gun and another pulled his wallet out and showed the detective the permit.

"It hasn't been fired, lieutenant," said the officer who had Jason's gun.

"My friend's parents were shot here in their garage," Jason began explaining. "Her name is Diamond Herrera. We were coming over to visit them. The garage door was open when we got here. We walked in and found that her mother and father had been shot multiple times. I have army medical training and I was treating a wound to the father's femoral artery. The EMT's said they both should survive. Di left in the ambulance with her mother."

"Did you see anyone leaving when you were driving up?" asked Bardo.

Jason hesitated for just a moment. "A white Ford Econoline sped past us about two blocks before we got here."

"Were you able to get a look at who was inside?"

"No. I didn't pay attention," answered Jason.

One of the officers was unrolling yellow crime scene tape, cordoning off the entire driveway and front yard. Another was placing numbered evidence markers next to each spent shell casing on the driveway.

"Has your friend, Diamond, mentioned anything about her parents being in any trouble?" asked the detective.

"Actually, Di is a former student of mine at Florida IT. We had just become reacquainted a couple of days ago. I had never met her parents ... before today."

"Why were you two coming here today?"

"Di is working on a story – I'm a journalism professor – and she wanted to meet to get some advice on it. We had lunch near here and Di wanted to come by and get something."

"Is that your Jeep?" asked Bardo.

"Yes."

"Where is your friend's vehicle?"

"At my condo in Cooper City," answered Jason.

Bardo scratched his ear. "So, she drove to your condo to get your expert advice. Then you decided to go out to lunch, but she left her vehicle at your place. Where did you eat lunch?"

"Actually, we hadn't eaten yet," said Jason. "We were going out to lunch and Di decided she wanted stop by here first."

"Thirty seconds ago you told me you had lunch near here," said Bardo.

"I must have mis-spoke," said Jason. "We were going to go to lunch near here but hadn't eaten yet.

"Where were you *going* to eat lunch, Mr. Taylor?"

"We hadn't decided yet," said Jason. "But we were heading in this direction and Di said she knew of a few good places near where she and her parents lived. That's when she said she wanted to stop by here."

"What was the story about that your friend wanted your help with?"

"She's working on a story about the immigrant asylum seekers who are being separated from their children at the border," said Jason.

"And you were helping her how?"

"How to get it in front of the right story editors, research ideas, those kinds of things."

"How were you helping her with research?" asked Bardo.

"Actually, she had already come up with excellent research sources on her own," said Jason.

"But you just said she was coming to you for help with research ideas."

"She did, but I pointed out to her that I couldn't think of any research sources that would be better than what she had come up with on her own."

"I suppose that could be considered help," said Bardo.

"Can I go?" asked Jason. "I really want to get changed out of these clothes and go to the hospital to be with Di and see how her folks are."

"Deputy Baez will follow you to your home and come in and take the clothes and shoes you're wearing for evidence," said Bardo. "Don't worry, you're not under suspicion. It's just procedure. He'll give you back your gun there. I'm going to the hospital, too, when I'm done here … we can all talk more then."

As soon as he was on his way Jason pulled out his black phone and called Di. He hoped she had hers with her.

She answered. "Jason, I'm sorry I went off on you. I don't blame you for what happened. Do you forgive me?"

"There's nothing to forgive, Di. I understand. Are you somewhere where you can listen carefully to me?"

"Yes. Mom and dad are in surgery. They told me they're both going to be okay."

"That's great news," said Jason. "When the cops showed, up a Detective Bardo questioned me. He'll be on his way to the hospital to talk to you. I'm going home to change, then I'll be there, too. Anyway, I told him you and I were going out to get lunch after you came to my place to get help with your story. Before we stopped for lunch you wanted to stop by your folks' place to get something. That's when we found them. It's important that you tell him the same thing – that we *had not* stopped for lunch, yet."

"I've got it," said Di. "We had not had lunch yet."

"I also told him that we saw the white Ford van speed by us about two blocks from your house. I told him I did not get a look at anyone inside, though."

"Anything else?" asked Di.

"I told him that you are a former student and you came to me two days ago for help with a story you were writing about immigrant children being separated from their parents. You wanted help with editor contacts and research, but I told you your research was already excellent. One more thing, I did not tell him anything about last night, Everglades or the children."

"I understand," said Di. "I hope you can get here soon."

"I think you still have a change of clothes at my place. I'll bring them."

"Thanks," said Di, trying not to look at her mother's blood on her white top that she had worn for Jason. "I was going to ask you to do that. Anything else?"

"I hate to ask you this, but it would save both of us a lot of grief if your parents did not tell anyone that we warned them," said Jason. "They could have just gone out to the garage to look for something and opened the door so they could see better."

"God, this is a nightmare," said Di. "I'll do my best. When can you get here?"

"Shouldn't be more than a half hour," said Jason.

CHAPTER 17

———∿∿∿———

Victor pulled up in front of the fourplex and hurried over to Rico to tell him the news. The left side of Victor's face was still purple and swollen from the night before. Rico was sitting in a folding chair outside his front door carving Our Lady of Guadalupe out of a block of wood with his Piranha auto knife.

"We got both of them, uncle," Victor announced with pride. "The bitch *and* the dude that was with her last night. The silencers worked great, just like you said."

"Anybody see you?" asked Rico.

"No. Their street was empty. It only took about thirty seconds."

"So, you did something right," said Rico. "Maybe there's hope for you in this life, nephew. Take your guns over to Enrique's. He'll give you three clean ones."

"Cross said she'd give us a full load of kids for offing those two," said Victor. "I'll call her and see when we can pick them up. I told you I'd make this right."

"Don't get ahead of yourself, nephew," said Rico as he continued carving. "You're only halfway there."

Victor called Rebecca as he and the two DK's walked to Enrique's to trade their guns.

"What is it, Victor?" she answered.

"I got rid of the two that stole the kids last night," he said. "When can I make the next pickup?"

"How do I know you got rid of them?"

"You doubt me?" he asked. "Watch the news tonight."

"I will," she answered. "We'll talk after I confirm it." She hung up.

Stupid bitch, thought Victor. She doesn't believe me.

Rebecca wasn't the only one that wanted confirmation. Rico checked the local news on his phone. There was nothing on the shooting yet.

When Jason arrived at the intensive care floor of All Souls Hospital he soon spotted Lieutenant Bardo interviewing Di in a waiting room. He walked in and handed her a bag containing her change of clothes and gave her a hug. Bardo greeted him and said he would like a few more minutes to speak with Di alone. Jason found a chair outside the room and waited. He knew Bardo would want to interview John and Robin as soon as it was possible.

A few minutes later he heard Bardo talking to someone on his phone. After the lieutenant hung up he told Di he had to go respond to another incident but that he would be back later to get statements from her parents. He also asked her to change into the clothes Jason had brought as he would have to take what she was wearing. There was a ladies' restroom next to the visitors waiting room. Di went in and quickly returned with the clothes in the bag and handed it to Bardo.

"So much for that outfit," she said to Jason as Bardo walked away. They went back into the empty waiting room and sat down.

Di turned to Jason and took his hand. "If we're not going to tell the police what really happened you're going to have to kill them," she said, barely audible.

Jason did not respond.

"If you don't they're just going to try again," she said. "Maybe they'll end up shooting more innocent people, but they'll eventually get us. Maybe Tommy and his guys will help you."

Jason finally spoke. "No, if I do this I'll do it alone. I should have finished them last night. If I had, none of this would have happened."

Jason was slowly beginning to think like a Ranger again. Innocent people needed protecting: Di, her parents, Reina, her brother and those kids locked up at Everglades.

A wall-mounted TV was on with the sound off in the waiting room. The four p.m. early local news had just started. Di looked up and was shocked to see photos of her parents – the headshots they had on their business website.

"Jason, quick, see if you can turn that up."

Jason found the remote and turned the sound on.

"The victims were John and Robin Herrera," the news broadcaster said. "Police have said that the married couple were shot in their garage earlier today on Foxtail Drive in Dania Beach. Though seriously wounded, both are expected to survive. Police have no suspects at this time and there do not seem to have been any witnesses. More on this story at six."

"Here we go," said Di. "Now they're going to know it wasn't us they shot and they'll be back."

"Di," said Jason. "That's a great idea."

"What's a great idea?"

"That they'll come back to your parents' house looking for you. Except they'll find me."

Just then the surgeon who had been operating on John entered the room. He told them that no organs had been hit, he repaired the artery and sewed up the other two wounds. He said that John would fully recover and that he would be awake and they could see him in two or three hours.

Di thanked him, thanked god and then she and Jason went back to planning.

"I'll make sure that my dad, and then my mom, know what to say to Bardo when he comes back," said Di. "What are you going to do?"

"I'm going to your house to wait," Jason said. He pulled out his Jeep keys and a valet ticket and handed them to Di. "I'm going to leave my Jeep for you. I parked it with the valet at the main entrance. Give me your keys. I'll take an Uber to my place and drive your car to your folks. We can't risk them recognizing the Jeep. If something does happen our story will be that I went to get your car for you. You had asked me to stop by your house to get some things for your parents and I just happened to be there when the shooters came back."

"I like it," said Di. She put her arms around Jason's neck and kissed him on the mouth and then said, "Be careful, Jason. Come back to me in one piece." Then she kissed him again. "Go."

As Jason rode in the back of the Uber down Stirling Road toward his condo he wondered if the fools that shot Robin and John would be so stupid as to come back on the same day looking for Di. He doubted it. Still, he would go there, turn on the lights in the front rooms and wait for a while before returning to the hospital. His Beretta had been returned to him by Deputy Baez and was back in his belt holster under his shirt.

He was impressed that Di had been aware enough to recognize, and verbalize, that they were in a kill or be killed situation.

One hour later, arriving at the Herrera home, Jason parked Di's Prius on the street. He wanted to keep the driveway clear in case the gangbangers returned. He let himself in with Di's key, turned on the lights – though it was still light out – helped himself to a beer from their fridge and positioned himself in a living room chair with a good view of the street and driveway.

Rico's wife, Carlotta, liked to watch the news. Rico couldn't care less what was going on outside their neighborhood. He was walking through their living room, though, as the news about the Herrera shooting was airing. It stopped him in his tracks.

"Rewind that story to the beginning," he told Carlotta.

Rico watched the story, saw the photos of John and Robin and thought, "Those can't be the people who took the kids."

"Miguel," he called out. Miguel came out from his bedroom.

"Go get Victor and bring him here," Rico told him.

"Rewind that news story to the beginning, then pause it," he told Carlotta.

Victor soon entered. "Nephew," said Rico. "Come over here. I want you to watch something."

Rico started the news story. "Those are the people you shot?" he asked Victor.

Victor was looking intently at the TV and the photos of Robin and John.

"Yeah, I guess so," said Victor.

"But those aren't the people who took the kids, are they?" Rico asked, his voice rising.

"Now that I see them more closely, I guess not," said Victor.

Rico's face was turning red. Carlotta could tell he was trying to control himself.

"You're done, Victor," Rico said, getting face-to-face with his nephew. Victor backed up a step. "You're through," Rico continued. "Go get a job on a taco truck. No more jobs for you. No more money from me."

Victor looked like a whipped dog.

"Get out of my sight, Victor. It's making me sick looking at you."

Victor had nothing to say. He left.

Back at his place, Victor began pacing rapidly. He started smacking himself on the uninjured side of his head, saying, *"Idiota, idiota, idiota,"* over and over.

His only hope, he thought, was to make this right … and soon. He had to go back. He couldn't use Rico's van. He didn't have his own car.

"Maria," he called out. "I need to use your car." Maria came out from a back room holding her baby.

"I need to go get some beer," he said to her. "And something for dinner. I won't be gone long."

Maria got her keys from her purse and gave them to Victor saying, "get me some wine."

Victor retrieved the replacement nine millimeter that Enrique had given him earlier and put it in the pocket of his low-slung baggy pants.

Victor got into Maria's old Honda Accord and took off … for Dania Beach. "I'll just drive by and see if anyone's there," thought Victor. "Since her parents are in the hospital, if anyone is there it has to be her … and maybe her boyfriend. If nobody's there I just turn around and leave."

It never occurred to Victor that Di would be at the hospital with her parents.

Jason was in the same chair, reading a magazine when Victor slowly drove by. Even though it wasn't the white van, Jason was immediately suspicious. He stood and slowly walked across the living room, past the picture window, so he could clearly be seen from the street.

Sure enough, the car turned around, came back toward the house and stopped in front of the driveway. The driver got out and slowly approached the house. Jason opened the door leading to the garage, pressed the garage door opener and crouched behind the first car. He did not turn on the garage light.

He could see it was Victor, with a gun in his hand. He was halfway up the driveway.

Jason suddenly stood and called out, "How's the head, amigo?"

Jason ducked back down as two bullets flew past and struck the wall behind him. He threw himself on the garage floor, between the two cars, drew a bead on the advancing Victor and fired three quick shots. Each hit Victor in the chest and he went down. Jason pulled his phone from his pocket and was dialing 911 as he approached the lifeless Victor.

Since Victor had shot first, Jason knew that his return fire was completely justified under Florida's Stand Your Ground law.

Jason was standing in nearly the same spot as he was when the police arrived earlier in the day. He laid his weapon on the ground and raised his hands when the first sheriff's car arrived. He had explained the situation to the 911 operator so, hopefully, the arriving police knew it was self-defense.

More sheriff's cars soon arrived and the scene played out much as it had earlier in the day. The first officer told Jason he could put his hands down as he asked him preliminary questions.

As Jason expected, Lieutenant Bardo pulled up a few minutes later.

"Looks like you got one of them," said Bardo.

"Ms. Herrera asked me to come over and pick up some things for her parents," Jason told him. "I observed this Honda drive by slowly, then turn around and park where you see it. I came into the garage and opened the door. The driver had gotten out and was approaching the house. As soon as he saw me he fired two shots. They should be in the back wall of the garage. I returned fire."

Bardo had checked Victor's gun and could tell it had been fired. "Looks like self-defense to me," he said.

"Completely," said Jason.

"You told me earlier that you were in the army. Which unit?"

"75th Ranger Regiment," replied Jason.

"Special Forces, eh? You're a hell of a shot," said Bardo.

"They trained us well," said Jason. "Do you mind if I lock up and head back to the hospital?"

"You can lock everything but the garage," said Bardo. "We'll need to dig out those slugs and take some photos. They'll close the garage door and go out the side when they're done."

An ambulance had arrived and the EMT's were loading Victor's body into it. A tow truck was hooking up Maria's Honda to be taken in for evidence.

A TV news crew had shown up and was trying to get Lt. Bardo to come over and give them a statement. He told Jason he would see him later at the hospital. Jason went back in, got the Herrera's personal items, locked the front door and got in the Prius. He had to drive over a few lawns to get around all the vehicles.

He pulled out his black phone and called Di.

"One down," he said, after she answered.

"You're kidding," Di exclaimed. "tell me what happened."

Jason told her it was the van driver from the night before, described what happened, asked about her parents, then told her he would be there in a few minutes.

Maria was getting worried. Victor had been gone for more than an hour. She walked next door to Rico's.

"Rico," she said to him. "Victor took my car to get groceries over an hour ago and he's not back yet. I'm getting worried. Do you know if he was going somewhere else?"

Rico paused, thinking. "I don't know. My nephew is unpredictable." He turned around. "Carlotta, keep watching that news. Let me know if there's anything I should see."

"You go home, Maria. I'm sure Victor will be back soon," he said.

Maria had not been gone two minutes when Carlotta called out, "Rico, come quick. I think it's about Victor. I'll rewind it."

"Incredibly," said the newscaster, "There has been a second shooting at a home in Dania Beach. We go there now, live."

"That's right," said the on-scene reporter. "We're told that a family friend came here to the Herrera home to retrieve items for John and Robin Herrera who are currently at All Souls Hospital being treated for gunshot wounds they received here earlier. It is believed that one of the shooters from earlier today returned to the home, attempted to make entry and was confronted by the family friend. The assailant fired first, the family friend, who has a licensed conceal carry permit, returned fire, killing the assailant. The police have told us that this was a clear case of Stand Your Ground self-defense."

One of the shots they showed was of Victor's body being loaded into the ambulance with the sheet pulled over his head.

"Do you think that's Victor?" asked Carlotta.

"Who else do you think would be so stupid as to go back over there?" replied Rico. "Now the cops will be over here questioning Maria, questioning me. He probably had his phone with him, too. *Mierda!*"

CHAPTER 18

Di's brain was working overtime while she waited for Jason and for her parents to come out of recovery. She researched separated immigrant children on her iPad. More than a few recent news articles she read told of how the U.S. Attorney General, frustrated by the public outcry and the government's lack of documentation on the families that had been separated, told the ACLU and Catholic Charities that if they could do a better job reuniting children with family members to go ahead and do whatever they could.

Di took this statement literally as she began considering different possible plans to reunite the children at Everglades. Reina, she thought, seemed to have little trouble finding temporary safe shelter for the 10 kids that they had freed. Could the same be done for all the children at Everglades if they could somehow get them out? In Jason, she already had a special forces expert experienced in freeing captives.

She phoned Reina. "Di," Reina answered. "I saw the news about your parents. I'm so sorry. I would have called you right away but I didn't want to bother you at the hospital. Are they going to be alright?"

Reina was at home preparing for a showing of her sculptures that weekend at a gallery in Boca Raton. She had missed the later story about Jason's encounter with Victor.

"Thanks, Reina," Di said. "The doctors said they should both make a full recovery."

"Well, one saving grace is that you weren't there," said Reina. "Do you think they'll come back?"

"One of them did come back," said Di. "Jason killed him."

"What?" exclaimed Reina.

Di described how Jason had gone to the home to pick up things for her parents and what had happened.

"Oh my god," said Reina. "I can't believe this. Was he hurt? Is he in trouble?"

"No," said Di. "He's okay, and the cops saw it was self-defense since the gangbanger shot first. That's not why I'm calling, though. I have a question for you. What if we were able to get all one-hundred-sixty-some kids out of Everglades. How could we pick them all up? Could we find people to take them all while their family members are located?"

"Wow," said Reina. "You think big. I don't know. I'll have to think about that. I could run it by my ACLU contact. He would maintain confidence. That would be a hell of a rescue, sister. God knows, the kids need to be taken out of there. How would you do that?"

"I don't know yet," said Di. "But I have a vision of a line of buses pulled up to Everglades and all the children filing out, getting on the buses and being taken to another location from where they can be dispersed to safehouses and church sanctuaries."

"Have you thought about how the sheriff's department or ICE would react to this?" Reina asked her. "It seems to me that whoever was involved would probably end up in jail. That's a high price to pay."

"I need to brainstorm about this with Jason," said Di. "I'm thinking we might have some leverage, though, with Everglades management."

After hanging up with Di, Reina figured it couldn't hurt to call her ACLU contact in Miami, Jim Jeffries. Jeffries, an ACLU veteran, was somewhat of a legend within the organization. The Harvard Law graduate was in his early sixties, tanned and with a full head of unruly silver hair. He had been with the ACLU for nearly forty years and had used his seniority to swing a transfer to the Miami office a few years earlier. As a passionate defender of the underdog, he had tried and won numerous precedent-setting cases during his career.

"Jim," Reina said when he answered. "This is Reina Suarez with the Immigrant Support group. I hope I'm not disturbing you."

"Not at all, Reina," said Jeffries. "I was just waiting in the office for this squall to pass so I can leave without getting drenched. What's on your mind?"

"Are you familiar with the Everglades Detention Facility here in Broward County?"

"Vaguely," Jeffries replied. "Why do you ask?"

"Well, they are owned and run by the DCA Group. There are slightly more than 160 kids there. My brother worked there until two days ago. It's a problem facility, Jim."

"How so, Reina?"

"Children there are being routinely drugged, there have

been two suicides … that we know of. My brother tells me there is abuse going on, both by the guards and by unsupervised older kids. But that's not the worst. I have proof that the facility manager is selling children to human traffickers."

Jeffries sat back down at his desk. "Oh my god," he said. "You say you have proof? What kind?"

"Some friends of mine were surveilling Everglades last night. To their surprise traffickers pulled up to the back of the facility. They observed the director – her name is Rebecca Cross – and a guard lead ten children out of the facility and into the back of the traffickers' van. They probably told them they were being taken to their parents or other family."

"Just observing isn't proof," Jeffries interrupted.

"There's more," Reina continued. "After the van left the facility, my friends stopped it, subdued the two traffickers and took the van and the children. Before they pulled away one of them took a photo that included the two traffickers, the children inside the van and the license plate. We already placed the children in safe houses and are working on locating their family members."

"That's incredible!" said Jeffries, clearly astounded.

"That's not all," said Reina. "One of the friends who rescued the children shot and killed one of the traffickers about an hour ago. It was self-defense. The trafficker was trying to exact revenge and shot first."

Jeffries was at a rare loss for words. "That's incredible," he repeated. "Are the police investigating the trafficking? Have they taken the facility chief into custody?"

"No," said Reina. "My friends were worried that informing law enforcement of what happened could put them in jeopardy. Their main concern was getting the kids to a safe place."

"I see," said Jeffries. "How can I help?"

"I think any caring person would agree that the children at Everglades need to be removed, for their safety," said Reina.

"If you have enough evidence about the abusive conditions there, and the two deaths, we could file a lawsuit demanding they be investigated and shut down."

"Okay, but that would take time," said Reina. "And even if you were able to shut it down, the kids would just be sent to another DCA facility where they would likely experience the same problems."

"Tell me what you are thinking," Jeffries asked.

"We have leverage over the facility chief because of her involvement in the trafficking," said Reina. "Say we use that leverage, plus a little trickery, to walk all of those kids out of there, load them on buses and then disperse them to safe houses and sanctuary while we locate their family members. What could the legal exposure be for those organizing or participating in this?"

"If I hear you right, you're asking if, legally speaking, the end can justify the means in such a situation," said Jeffries. "It's called consequentialism in the law."

"Didn't the Attorney General recently say that the government was giving permission for the ACLU and religious organizations to take their own actions in reuniting separated families since the government did not seem up to it?" asked Reina.

"Yes, he did," said Jeffries. "But his directive was generally understood to mean research, legal and travel assistance … not breaking immigrant children out of federally contracted detention facilities."

"You say breaking them out," said Reina. "I say rescuing them from abuse, and worse. Bottom line, Jim, can we count on the ACLU's help if this is done?"

"I would need to get more facts about the situations you've described. I would like to meet with you, your two friends, your brother, and anyone else involved."

"Are you available tomorrow?" Reina asked. "If the others can make it we could all meet at my place in Pembroke Pines. I'm just off 75." She gave him her address.

"If it's early to mid-morning I can make it," said Jeffries.

"Thanks, Jim," said Reina. "Let's tentatively set it for nine-thirty. I'll confirm with the others and get back to you."

Reina then phoned Father Pat Sullivan from Catholic Charities, described the situation to him and asked if he could attend the meeting. Father Pat had already been told some of the stories of abuse after talking with the kids he had picked up earlier. He was a young, progressive, multi-lingual priest and was intrigued by the possibility of being able to begin the reunification process for so many immigrant children at once. He, too, was interested in the ACLU's take on whether the extraction of these children for their own protection could be legal.

CHAPTER 19

⎯⎯⎯⎯⎯

A ntonio awoke to a cockroach crawling on his face on his sixteenth day of incarceration at Everglades. He swatted it off and it scurried off toward the still-sleeping boy next to him. Only two of the guards spoke Spanish … and not very well. He had been told nothing about his asylum request, how long he would be there or the whereabouts of Isabella. Through one of the boys who spoke some English, he asked the guards if someone could contact his aunt in Houston, telling them that he could stay with her while his case was being considered. He was told they were not authorized to do that.

Antonio was eager to learn English. A flat-screen TV mounted on the wall outside the cage was tuned to an English language Christian channel from eight a.m. until eight p.m. Although he would watch it intently now and then, the only word he recognized was, "Jesus." He also had gotten a beat-up Louis Lamour paperback from a box of donated books, but he couldn't make anything out of that, either. A few of the boys in his cage knew a little English and would try to teach others, like Antonio, who were interested in learning.

Adalberto had calmed down since their sandwich and milk confrontation. They had even become almost friends.

There were a few other boys there from Honduras, as well as boys from El Salvador, Guatemala, Mexico, and even Cuba. During their long days with nothing to do, the boys compared stories of their journeys to the border, their experiences crossing it and about their home towns. Most had made the trip with a parent. Some, like Antonio, had made the trip with a sibling. All had been separated from their accompanying family members.

Antonio and two of the other older boys had emerged as leaders within the group, taking it upon themselves to maintain order, befriend and counsel the younger boys and set a positive example.

The girls' cage was twenty-five feet away from the boys and most days the closest side of each enclosure was lined with boys and girls calling out to each other, teasing and flirting.

Two port-a-potties had been brought into each cage because the guards got tired of having to unlock the door every time a child had to go to the bathroom. The only time they got to wash was during once-a-week showers.

Each morning the nurse would come around with pills they would have to take. Antonio didn't know what they were. They were told that they were vitamins ... *vitaminas*, but he just knew they made him sleepy.

Most of the children who arrived before Antonio were housed in another part of the facility in an open, dorm-like area with rows of narrow steel bunkbeds. The boys were on one side of the long room and the girls on the other, with a curtain divider between them. This is where the boy-on-girl abuse was occurring at night. Boys who were caught assaulting girls were put in isolation: small, bare rooms with just a cot, a thin blanket and a stainless steel toilet.

There was no one on staff at Everglades working to find the children's family members who were either detained elsewhere or living legally in the U.S. and offering to house them. Nor was anyone there monitoring their asylum cases in immigration court.

Those things were handled by DHS, who would contact Everglades if there was a change in a child's status. Not many children had left Everglades since Antonio had arrived. Although he had been heartened to see ten children leaving to be reunited a couple of nights earlier. He envied them.

CHAPTER 20

Lt. Grady Bardo, forty years old, had been with the Broward County Sheriff's Department for fifteen years. He had risen through the ranks from patrol cop to senior robbery and homicide investigator. His favorite TV cop was Peter Falk's Lt. Colombo. He had Colombo's "One more thing" routine down pat and was continually disappointed that no interviewee had yet recognized and complimented him on it. Since the South Florida climate wasn't conducive to daily raincoat wearing, his preferred attire was a well-pressed tropical shirt with linen dress slacks. He wore his dark hair in a curly texture cut that was set of with a goatee flecked with premature gray.

At home, Bardo liked to tell his two kids, a boy and a girl, ages twelve and fourteen, that he was more into peace and quiet than law and order.

Bardo took pride in being one-eighth Seminole Indian. His father's father's father was Billy Bardo, a full-blooded Seminole. His great grandfather's family, along with a few others, had evaded the final relocation of the Seminoles from Florida to Oklahoma in 1842 and lived for three generations as nomads in the Everglades.

In the early part of the twentieth century Billy, and other Seminoles, began working in the sugar cane fields for the newly-formed Florida Sugar and Food Products Company. William Greenwood, one of the three founders of the company, took a liking to Billy and became his mentor. Billy went on to earn a degree in agriculture from the University of Miami, where he met Bardo's great grandmother.

Bardo worked out of the Dania Beach district office. Since he was the first detective on the scene at the Herrera home, he was assigned to investigate both shootings. The dead shooter was ID'd as Victor Valbuena, a member of the Dominican Kings gang. But the DK's territory was in Allapattah, more than twenty miles from Dania Beach. What could they have to do with a couple of suburban CPA's? He had learned that the Herrera's owned an accounting business. Could they have been laundering money for the DK's? And how did this journalism professor, Jason Taylor, fit in?

Bardo would soon be back at All Soul's. The Herrera's should be out of recovery by now. He would interview the four of them separately. Meanwhile, the dead DK's phone was being analyzed. Hopefully, that would provide some answers.

Jason was in the family waiting room when Bardo arrived. Di was with her father, who was now out of recovery and in a double room where Robin would soon be joining him. She was prepping him to not reveal to the police that she and Jason had phoned to warn them. They had only phoned to say they were stopping over. John was still a little out of it due to the surgery and the pain medication, but he assured her he understood.

"How are the Herrera's doing?" Bardo asked Jason who had stood to greet him.

"Their doctors said that John will recover fully," said Jason. "They said that Robin will require additional surgery on her lung as soon as she is strong enough."

"Why do you think they were targeted?" asked Bardo.

"I don't know," answered Jason.

"Do you think it could have anything to do with the story Ms. Herrera is working on about separated immigrant children?"

"I really don't know. I guess anything is possible."

Just then Bardo's phone rang. It was Stacy, his department's phone evidence analyst.

"Lieutenant, we got something interesting off Victor Valbuena's phone. He made four calls over the past two weeks to the Everglades Detention Facility."

"Maybe he knows someone who is being held there," said Bardo.

"That's what I was thinking at first, but the calls went to the administrator's direct line, not to their main public number," said Stacy. "Also, this same administrator called Valbuena from her cell phone earlier today."

"Good work," said Bardo. "What is the administrator's name?"

"Rebecca Cross," replied Stacy.

"Got it," said Bardo. "Let me know if you find anything else interesting."

He turned back to Jason. "What do you know about the

Everglades Detention Facility and Rebecca Cross? Do they play a part in the story Ms. Herrera is writing?"

"I know that Di took part in a demonstration at that facility earlier this week," said Jason. "She also did some volunteer translating there a couple of days ago. Who is Rebecca Cross?"

"She's the administrator of Everglades," said Bardo. "We found her office number and cell number on the phone of the gangbanger you shot."

"Di told me she interviewed a former employee of Everglades this week who told her, among other things, that he suspected that the children detained there were being drugged and abused."

"Well, unless Mr. and Mrs. Herrera were the target of the Dominican Kings shooters – and I doubt they were – then your friend, Ms. Herrera, must have been the target," said Bardo. "It's possible they mistook Mrs. Herrera for her daughter. And they shot Mr. Herrera to eliminate a witness. Somehow, they later realized their mistake and one of them came back looking for Ms. Herrera. Do you know where she is? I have some questions for her."

"She's with her father in the room he was assigned," said Jason. "I'll walk you down there."

Di heard the soft knock on the door, turned and saw Jason with Lt. Bardo. She touched her dad's arm. "I'll be back soon, dad. It looks like the detective wants to talk to me."

"Hello again Ms. Herrera," said Bardo, as Di came out into the hall. "I hope your parents will be alright."

"Thank you, Lieutenant," said Di. "The doctors say they should both recover. My mother will need more work done on her lung."

"I'm truly sorry to hear that," said Bardo. "I have a few more questions I need to ask. Do you mind if we go to the waiting room?"

"I'm happy to do anything I can to help solve this," said Di.

Once they were seated in the waiting room Bardo asked Di what she could tell him about Everglades and Rebecca Cross. Di was surprised that these were the first questions the Lieutenant asked.

She told him about the demonstration, meeting Chief Cross the next day and translating, as well as her interview of Tomas.

"Why would any of this cause these gang members to try to kill me?" she asked.

"My guess is that Rebecca Cross, for some reason, decided that you posed a threat," said Bardo. "She may have found out that you had interviewed the former employee and feared you had learned too much from him and/or from the children you interviewed when you were translating. I still don't know how the Dominican Kings gang is involved. I find it hard to believe that she would order a hit on you just because of a suspicion. The DK's may have decided on their own to take it to that level."

"Lieutenant," Di said. "My source also told me that two of the children hanged themselves and are probably buried out behind the facility. Given what's going on out there, isn't there some way to get those children out and moved to somewhere safe?"

"I'm afraid that's above my pay grade," said Bardo. "It's my understanding that the DCA Group has a sweetheart relationship with Homeland Security. Any investigation of their operations would be conducted by DHS. Honestly, I would be surprised if anything came of it."

"You mean *you* can't investigate them as part of this case?" asked Jason.

"The Broward County Sheriff has no jurisdiction at that facility," answered Bardo. "In fact, if I want to interview Cross I'll have to catch her at her home or somewhere else other than on DCA property."

"That's unbelievable," said Di.

"I've got the address for the DK that Mr. Taylor shot today. After I see if your father can give me descriptions I'm going to head over there with a Miami-Dade County detective and see what I can find out," said Bardo.

He got Tomas's contact information from Di before standing to leave.

"I'll be in touch with you about what I find out," said Bardo. "In the meantime, Ms. Herrera, I would strongly recommend that you find somewhere else to stay for at least a few days until we determine that you are no longer at risk at your parents' home."

"I will definitely do that," said Di, sneaking a sideways look at Jason.

"He seems like a nice guy," Di said to Jason after Bardo had left.

"I hope he is," said Jason. "Come on, let's go see if your mom is in with your dad yet."

Just then Di's phone rang. It was Reina asking if she and Jason could come to her place the next morning to meet with Jim Jeffries, an ACLU attorney, Father Pat and her to discuss the legality of removing all the children from Everglades.

Di confirmed with Jason that he wanted to attend, got her address and told Reina they would both be there.

CHAPTER 21

It was dark by the time Jason and Di turned their vehicles onto Jason's street and saw the TV news van parked in front of his condo. As Jason pulled into his garage and Di pulled into his driveway behind him the reporter, her cameraman and lighting person exited the van and set up in Jason's driveway.

"We're here at the home of today's Stand Your Ground shooter, Jason Taylor," the reporter said into her microphone.

Jason got out of his Jeep and waited in the garage for Di.

"Mr. Taylor, Mr. Taylor, can you talk to us about today's shooting?" the reporter called out, advancing toward the garage.

"No comment," Jason called back to her, just before closing the garage door.

Once inside the condo Di said, "That's the same reporter that was covering the demonstration at Everglades."

"She must have some excellent sources," said Jason. "I wonder how she got my address."

"Let's hope the Dominican Kings aren't watching the news," said Di.

They peered out through the blinds on Jason's front window. The cameraman was still shooting and the reporter was still talking.

"She's probably describing the shootings at my parents' house," said Di. "Can't we get them to leave?"

"It would just make things worse if I went out there," said Jason. "They'll be gone soon."

They walked away from the window and Jason headed for the kitchen. "I think I have a frozen pizza I can throw in the oven. You hungry?"

"I'm so hungry you might have to fight me for it," said Di.

"I've had enough fighting for one day," said Jason before going back into the garage to get more beer and water from his garage refrigerator. He pulled out two beers for he and Di before loading the bottles into his kitchen fridge.

"I'll throw this pizza in the oven and we can finally sit back and relax," he said.

He soon joined Di on his couch and turned on the Miami Marlins baseball game on his TV with the volume on low.

"So, I wonder where I can stay until this blows over?" Di asked.

"That's right," said Jason. "I had forgotten about that. There's a Days Inn not too far from here."

Di punched him in the arm. "*You* go stay at the Days Inn. I'm staying here."

"I charge a lot more than they do," said Jason.

"Don't worry, you'll get paid," said Di. She took his beer out of his hand, put both bottles on the coffee table turned his head toward her and suddenly they were making out on the couch.

Soon Di was on her back with Jason on top of her. Di moved her right hand to between Jason's thighs. She could feel him growing ... larger and harder, as they continued kissing. Di had been so focused on getting her career off the ground that she hadn't been serious with a man for many months. This felt right, though. It felt *very* right.

Although Jason ran into opportunities almost every day, he wasn't the kind of man who was into one-night stands. He knew now, though, as he kissed Di and felt her caress, that this was right for him as well. He wanted to call her baby ... honey, tell her that everything would be alright.

Instead he said, "I'd better check the pizza." Getting up he continued, "now that I think about it, I did see a no vacancy sign at the Days Inn when we drove by."

Di sat up, straightening her hair, "that's more like it."

She got up, bounded into the kitchen, leapt onto Jason's back and wrapped her arms around his neck, yelling, "pizza fight, pizza fight."

Jason pulled a Ranger move on her, bending over to roll her over his shoulder, stood her in front of him, holding one arm behind her back and started kissing her.

When they finally parted Di said, "You win. I'll give you half."

Jason checked the pizza, turned and said, "it needs about five more minutes," put his arms around Di and they were kissing again. Open mouths exploring. Jason's hands exploring.

Once they parted Di said, "please tell me we're sleeping together tonight."

Jason reached behind her, turned off the oven, took her hand and said, "we're sleeping together right now."

He started pulling her into the living room and toward his bedroom. She quickly passed him and was now pulling him toward his bedroom. Once in the room they tore their clothes off and jumped on top of Jason's bed, rocking and rolling like a couple of new lovers.

Nearly an hour later they lay next to each other, sweating, still breathing heavily, exhausted. Neither spoke. Finally, Jason turned toward her and began running his finger slowly along her gleaming skin, starting at her neck, down between her beautiful breasts, down across her flat stomach, down to her closely trimmed strip, and below, then down her brown thigh. He was burning every inch of her into his memory.

Di watched and felt his hand and thought, "*this* is a man, this is *the* man, I want him to be *my* man."

"It might not be safe for me to leave for quite a while," she finally said, softly.

"I was thinking the same thing," replied Jason.

CHAPTER 22

Since Little Santo Domingo was in Miami-Dade County, Lt. Bardo had arranged for one of their sheriff's detectives, Lt. Monique Escobar, to accompany him to the late Victor's address. The sun was close to setting as he knocked on Maria's door. When she answered she was holding an infant and he could see that her eyes were still red.

"I'm Lieutenant Bardo from Broward County and this is Lieutenant Escobar with Miami-Dade County," said Bardo as they held their badges up. "We're here about Victor Valbuena."

"My Victor was murdered today, wasn't he?" asked Maria, beginning to cry again.

"Not exactly," Bardo replied. "You're Maria Diaz?" Maria nodded while dabbing her face with a tissue with her free hand. "Victor drove your vehicle to a residence in Dania Beach and began shooting at one of the occupants. The occupant returned fire and killed Victor. Your vehicle is being held by the Broward County Sheriff as evidence. We will notify you when that process is complete and you can come get it. That will probably take a few weeks."

"Do you mind if we come in and ask you a few questions?" Lt. Escobar asked her in Spanish.

Maria held the door open and they entered. "Does Victor keep any weapons here?" asked Bardo.

"I don't think so. I don't know. Anyway, you guys don't have a search warrant."

"Is anyone else here?" asked Bardo, looking down the hall.

"Just me and this one. What are they going to do with Victor's body?"

"Actually, we would like you to come down and provide an official identification," said Bardo. "Unless there is another family member you would rather have do the ID."

"Where's Rico?" asked Escobar. Her sector of Miami-Dade County included Allapattah and she was well acquainted with Victor's uncle and many of the other DK's.

"I don't know. He doesn't check in with me."

"Where was Victor going when he left in your car?" Bardo asked.

"He said he was going out for groceries."

"Where was he between noon and one today?"

"I don't know. Hey, I'm in mourning. I'd like to be left alone."

"Who owns the white van?" Bardo was fishing. The van was no longer out front. Rico had moved it after he learned of the botched first shooting.

"What white van?" asked Maria.

"The white van that Victor and his other two gang friends were driving when they shot up an innocent couple at the same house in Dania Beach between noon and one today."

"You can both go now," said Maria, walking toward the front door. "I'm done answering your questions."

"I'll need your full name and phone number so we can get back to you about your car," said Bardo, pulling out his notepad.

Maria put the baby on the floor, wrote down her information, and handed it to Bardo.

"Does the name Rebecca Cross mean anything to you?" Bardo asked.

"No." Maria was telling the truth. Cross had not identified herself when she called Victor on Maria's phone, and Victor had never mentioned Cross's name to her.

"She runs a detention facility for immigrant children in the Everglades," said Bardo. "If we find any calls to or from Cross when we search your phone records, that will implicate *you* in whatever Victor and she were involved in."

Maria had picked her baby up and was listening intently. She thought about Victor using her phone to call someone, and then a woman calling him. She now suspected that it was the Rebecca Cross that Bardo was talking about.

"I know that you want to remain a free woman so you can continue to raise your beautiful child," Bardo told her. "If you get tied into these attempted murders and whatever else Rebecca Cross and Victor were involved in you will go to prison for a long time and your child will be raised by foster parents. You should seriously think about cooperating with us. You can no longer get Victor in any trouble."

"I really don't know anything," Maria said. She leaned closer to Bardo and Escobar and said in a lowered voice, "Our men tell us nothing. We cook the meals, spread our legs, and raise the kids."

Bardo handed Maria his card. "If you think of anything at all, Maria, please call me."

Maria took the card, saying nothing. Bardo opened the door and he and Escobar walked out. A few steps down the walk, Bardo told Escobar, "hold on a minute." He walked back to the door, opened it and stuck his head in. "One more thing, Maria. Since Victor was driving your car during the attempted murder of Mr. Taylor, the Broward prosecutor might look into charging you as an accessory. Just something else to think about. Call me anytime."

The two had driven their own cars to Maria's. Walking back to them Bardo asked her if she could join him in his so he could get more background information on the Dominican Kings.

"If it's all the same to you lieutenant," she said. "I'd rather give you that information over the phone. And I would recommend you don't spend time in your car writing notes or phoning while you're sitting in front of this DK row house."

"Point well taken," said Bardo. "Thanks for joining me on this house call. I appreciate it."

"Good luck on your case. Call me anytime. And thank your citizen for ridding our world of Victor Valbuena."

Bardo called his office, gave them Maria's cell phone number and requested they get a warrant to search her phone records. They had gotten Cross's office and cell phone numbers when they searched Victor's phone. If either number was found in Maria's phone records he would go back and pick her up.

CHAPTER 23

———～～～———

Di was awakened by the high-pitched whine of a landscaper's weed wacker right outside Jason's bedroom window. It took her a couple of seconds to realize where she was. Then the memories of the night before came rushing back. She could feel where Jason had been and smiled. He was already up, showered, and doing classwork at his dining table. It was ten to eight on Saturday morning.

She found a white terrycloth robe in Jason's closet, put it on, ran her brush through her hair, checked her face and went out to join Jason.

"Good morning," said Jason. "Sorry about the weed wacker."

"That's okay. I needed to get up anyway." She went over, wrapped her arms around his neck and kissed him on the head. "Good morning to you."

Jason told her where to find the coffee pot and a cup.

"I need some different clothes," Di said. "All I have is what I've worn for two days now. I don't have time to drive to my parents and back before the meeting."

"That wouldn't be a good idea anyway," said Jason. "There's a Target over on Griffin Rd. about five minutes from here."

"Then that's where I'm going," said Di. She bent down and kissed Jason on the cheek. He turned and met her lips with his. After their lips parted, Di put her mouth to Jason's ear. "Last night was incredible," she whispered.

"I'm glad we're in agreement on that," said Jason.

"I feel guilty feeling so happy when my parents are in such bad shape. I need to go see them right after the meeting. But right now, I need to get dressed and go get something else to wear."

Di emerged from the bedroom five minutes later, kissed Jason again and left for Target.

Jason had his coursework spread out in front of him, but he couldn't concentrate on it. All he could think about was Di and their night together. "Get it together," he thought. They were both in the middle of what had turned out to be a deadly situation.

He thought about the upcoming meeting. What they learn there could settle a lot as to what their next move would be. He wondered if Tommy Ziker would want to be there. He picked up his phone and called him.

"Tommy ... Jason. Do you have a minute?"

"For you? Always, my brother. Say, I saw where you took down one of the DK traffickers yesterday. Score one for the good guys. You okay?"

"Yeah, I'm fine. Diamond's parents aren't, though."

"I heard about that, too. Tell Di my prayers are with them."

"Maybe you can tell her yourself. We're going to a meeting this morning with an ACLU immigration lawyer and a priest from Catholic Charities, along with Reina, who you met. It's at nine-thirty at Reina's house in Pembroke Pines. It'll be about whether it's possible or legal to remove all of the kids from Everglades and distribute them to safe houses and sanctuaries. I don't know if what will be discussed will be relevant to the work that you do, but I know that if what I've been thinking about goes down I could sure use your help."

"Jason, I gotta say, I'm pretty intrigued by what you've gotten yourself into. It kinda takes me back to our Ranger days. I'm sure not gonna bow out now. Plus, we've got to protect your woman, right? Give me the address. I'll be there."

"Thanks, Tommy. See you there."

Di wasn't gone long. She used Jason's shower, changed into her new shorts and top, got her face and hair ready and emerged from the bedroom.

Jason watched her approach. "Do you know you're glowing?" he asked her.

"Yeah? Well you've got a little glow going on yourself."

He got up and they kissed again.

"We should eat something before we go," he said. "I'm a master at toast. How do you like yours?"

"Medium well, with whatever kind of jam you have."

CHAPTER 24

The meeting attendees were assembled in Reina's living room by nine-forty. Reina started off by introducing everyone.

Jim Jeffries asked Tomas if he would describe for them what he knew about the goings on at Everglades.

Tomas repeated the stories that he had told Di about the drugging, the abuse, the suicides and the sale of kids.

When he was done, Father Pat spoke up, "I think it would be good if we all would say a silent prayer right now for the welfare of these separated, incarcerated children."

All bowed their head for a few moments.

It was Di who spoke first. "Mr. Jeffries, I think we're all wondering the same thing – is there a legal way to get those children out of that facility and work on reuniting them ourselves?"

"As I described to Reina," he said. "The fact that these children are being subjected to unlawful, abusive, life-threatening conditions could present a defense of the end justifying the means. But for those accused of such an act it would be an uphill road to prevail in court."

"Could the ACLU provide a defense for those who might be charged in such a rescue?" Di asked.

"I couldn't commit to that," said Jeffries. "Those kinds of decisions are made by the national committee."

"Father Pat, what is the possibility of pre-arranging safe shelter for more than one-hundred-sixty children until we can find their families and move them?" Reina asked. "Perhaps involving all the dioceses in Florida?"

"That's a tall order. I don't see how you could get all of the children out of there in a safe, orderly way."

Jason stood, took his phone out, brought up the photo he took of the van with Victor, Miguel and the ten children and showed it to Father Pat, then to Jeffries and Tomas.

"The administrator of Everglades is the inside person responsible for organizing the sale of children there to human traffickers," said Jason. "She knows that someone intercepted this load of children two nights ago. She doesn't know who did it, though. I'm thinking it might be possible to use the combination of a ruse, and her desire not to get charged with human trafficking, to walk all of those kids out of there and onto buses that then drive to another location, or locations, where other vehicles are waiting to take them, in smaller numbers, to safe shelter."

"I see what you're getting at," said Tommy. "If you had enough guys who were wearing Homeland Security-type windbreakers you could bluff your way inside, show the administrator your photo and tell her it would be in her best interest to cooperate in the transfer of all of the children. She then tells her staff that this is an order from Homeland Security so that they assist in getting the kids out. The buses pull up, load up and then it's up to the good Father and Reina's people to disperse and shelter them. What could go wrong?"

"Mr. Jeffries, what about the Attorney General's statement that the ACLU and church groups have the government's permission to get involved in the family reunifications," asked Di. "Couldn't that, along with the ends justifying the means, give us cover for something like this?"

"Possibly, but it would probably be a hell of a court battle ... sorry, Father."

"You're forgiven, sir."

"What if this was done in a way that no one involved could be identified?" asked Jason. "My school's theatre department has a makeup artist who can do things to a person's face that would make them unrecognizable to their mother, yet the disguise is natural, not obvious. *And*, he's a good friend of mine."

About this time, Jason and Tommy were having the same thought: how much of this should they be talking about in front of Tomas. He seemed like a good kid, and he was Reina's brother, but what if the DK's and Cross suspected he was the source of the trafficking information and they came after him? All the DK's would have to do is pick him up and squeeze him for what he knew.

Jason stood and walked toward Reina's kitchen, touching her shoulder as he went by and motioned for her to follow him.

Once in the kitchen he asked her, "Is there somewhere out of town that Tomas can go until this is all over? I don't think he's safe. Cross must have told the DK's about him, just like she did with Di."

He could tell Reina was thinking. "You're right," she said. "Tomas was just about to move out of his place, since he lost his job, and move in with me temporarily. We do have a sister living in Orlando. I'll call her and see if Tomas can visit for a while."

"I think that's the best thing," said Jason. "In fact, I'd get things moving today if you can."

"I will," she said, and they both returned to the group.

"Just to be sure," said Jason. "Are these conversations privileged? Father? Counselor?"

Both assured Jason and the others that attorney/client privilege and pastoral privilege prevented them from revealing any of their conversations.

As they all stood to leave, Father Pat said he would begin making inquiries regarding the transportation and sheltering of the kids. Jim Jeffries assured them he would research the laws and consult with his colleagues. Reina said she would also work on arranging shelter once her weekend gallery showing was over.

Reina asked Tomas to stay for a bit as the others left.

Jason, Tommy and Di walked to their vehicles together. "What do you think?" Jason asked Tommy.

"You know I'm a sucker for mass rescues while in disguise, don't you? Once you threw in makeup you had me."

"I'm glad Jason has you for a friend, Tommy," said Di. "He told me about how you and your guys handled the DK's yesterday. I wish I could have been there."

"After what Jason and I have been through together you develop a bond. Am I right, Jase?"

"You're right, Tommy. I wonder if any of the other guys live around here and would be interested in a little action?"

"I'll give it some thought," said Tommy. "Don't forget, I've got some pretty good guys, too. I'll be in touch."

Jason and Di drove back to his place. She left immediately for the hospital without coming in. "Too much temptation in there," she thought to herself and smiled.

CHAPTER 25

Rebecca Cross did not sleep well Friday night. She had seen the news the night before about Victor being killed. It made sense to her that the guy who shot Victor – this Jason Taylor they were reporting about – is the same one who took the kids. That means he's the one who took the photo Victor told her about.

And, both of her numbers are in Victor's phone, which the cops now have. She had spent a lot of time lying in bed trying to think of an explanation for that.

Lt. Bardo had that question in the front of his mind as he walked up to Rebecca's townhouse door and rang the bell.

She looked out her front window and saw his car parked outside. "Here we go," she thought.

"Yes?" she said, after opening the door.

"I'm Detective Lieutenant Bardo with the Broward County Sheriff's Department. Are you Rebecca Cross?"

"Yes."

"I have a few questions for you about a man who was shot and killed yesterday, a Victor Valbuena. Do you mind if I come in?"

"No. Yes, come in." Chief Cross was still in her robe, which was actually a floor-length red Japanese kimono, and holding a cup of coffee.

"Can I get you a cup of coffee … lieutenant was it?"

"Yes, that would be fine. Thank you."

"We can sit here," said Cross, motioning to the living room.

Bardo waited until she returned with the coffee before sitting.

"Did you know Mr. Valbuena?" he asked.

"I spoke with him a few times, but I didn't know him. One of my staff, a Captain Lopez, worked out at the same gym as he did. Mr. Valbuena was helping his cousin find a job. Captain Lopez gave him my number since our facility is expanding. He phoned me a few times regarding his cousin."

"What is the facility you refer to?" asked Bardo.

"The Everglades Detention Facility. It's just west of here. I'm the Chief Administrator. We house detained immigrants while their cases are being processed."

"I see. I wonder why Victor's cousin didn't phone you himself about the job?"

"Actually, he did, but he used Victor's phone."

"So, Victor phoned you a few times and then his cousin phoned you. How many times did the cousin phone you?"

"I don't know. Maybe two."

"The last call from Victor's phone to your office phone was at 11:00 p.m. two nights ago. Seems like an odd time to call the head of the facility about a job."

"Not really. My shift runs from four p.m. to midnight. Victor's cousin knew that."

"What's the cousin's name?"

"Ah, Manuel … I'm pretty sure. I deal with more than one hundred people with Hispanic names every day. It's hard to remember them all."

"So, if I talk to this Manuel, he'll confirm what you've told me?"

"If his memory works, he will."

"Why wouldn't his memory work?"

"I got the idea from Captain Lopez, and also from talking with them, that they may be drug users."

"Why do you think your captain would recommend someone directly to you, and give them your phone number, if he suspected the person of being a drug user?"

"That's a good question. I'll have to ask him that."

"What is Captain Lopez's full name?"

"Anthony Lopez."

"Do you have a home address and phone number for Captain Lopez?"

"Not here. I have them at my office. I'll be back there on Monday afternoon."

"Did anyone else from Victor Valbuena's family call you?"

"No."

"How about any friends of his?"

"No."

"Were you aware that Victor Valbuena was a member of the Dominican Kings gang?"

"No, I wasn't. I've never heard of them."

Bardo looked at his notepad and took a sip of his coffee.

"Mr. Valbuena called your cell phone yesterday. About

forty-five minutes after the first shooting at the Herrera's. What was that about?"

"Actually, that was Manuel again. I guess Captain Lopez gave Victor my cell phone number, too. That kid's become a real pest."

Bardo closed his notebook and stood. "You've been very helpful, Ms. Cross. Here is my card. If Manuel phones you again please call me and give me his number. He may have to get his own phone now that Victor's is no longer available to him."

Rebecca walked him to the door. "I will do that, Lieutenant."

"Actually, now that I think about it," said Bardo. "I'm going over to Victor's right now. Maybe I can find Manuel and talk to him myself."

"Perhaps. Good luck, lieutenant," said Rebecca, closing the door after him.

Just as the door was about to latch, it pushed back open.

"There's just one more thing," said Bardo, stepping halfway in. "Why would Victor want to kill Diamond Herrera?"

"That name sounds familiar."

"It should. She translated for you three days ago at your facility."

"That's right, now I remember her. I have no idea. It seems odd that they would know each other."

"You're right. Odd. Okay, that's all for now. Thank you again."

Bardo got back in his car thinking, "She acted cool on

the outside but I'll bet she was sweating bullets under that godawful kimono."

The only possible connection between Cross and the Dominican Kings serious enough to involve attempted murder of a witness would be human trafficking. That had to be it … Cross was selling kids to Victor Valbuena.

He wished he could go in and arrest her right now, but he needed more evidence.

Bardo had spoken on the phone with Lt. Escobar after their visit with Maria. She told him about Rico Valbuena, Victor's uncle and a captain in the Dominican Kings, and that Rico lived in the unit next to Victor.

"Then why the hell didn't she tell me that when we were both there," he thought at the time.

Now he had to call the Miami-Dade sheriff again and arrange for another detective to join him while he visited Rico. He hoped he would get someone more helpful than Escobar.

Miami-Dade couldn't provide someone until that afternoon, so he decided to go to All Souls again and talk with the Herreras. Hopefully, their daughter would be there, as well.

Di was sitting in her parents' room reading a magazine when Bardo arrived.

Robin was alert and able to answer questions now, although speaking was difficult for her due to her lung wound.

Both Robin and John told him the same story: that they went out to the garage to find a cooler and John had opened the garage door so they could see better.

"Why was it necessary for both of you to go get the cooler?" asked Bardo.

"You have to understand that Robin and I are a bit competitive with each other," said John. "Robin remembered the cooler being in one place and I recalled it being in another. We both hurried out to the garage in order to prove the other wrong."

"Right after John opened the door so we could see better, those men started shooting at us," added Robin in a strained voice.

"Can you give me any kind of description of the gunmen?"

"They had bandanas pulled up over their faces," Robin struggled to say. "One of them was shorter than the others."

"And they were wearing wrap-around sunglasses," added John.

"Well, we now believe that your daughter was their target," said Bardo. "But they had never seen her before and must have thought that Mrs. Herrera was Diamond. And they tried to kill Mr. Herrera so there would not be a witness."

"I'm so sorry mom, dad," said Di.

"It's not your fault, honey," said John. "The important thing now is that you stay safe until the others are caught."

Bardo went on, "I visited Rebecca Cross this morning. I now suspect that she was trafficking immigrant children from her facility to Victor Valbuena and the Dominican Kings. Cross probably believed that one of the children that Di interviewed, or Tomas Suarez, a former employee, told Di what was going on."

"So, they decided to murder our daughter on a hunch?" asked John.

"A human trafficker convicted in Florida is looking at twenty-five years in prison, minimum," said Bardo. "Life is cheap for these people, and murdering a witness elevates the status of the shooter within the gang. I've seen people killed for a lot less."

"Jason has been kind enough to let me stay with him for a while," Di said to her parents. "I can't think of anyone safer to be with."

"I have to agree with your daughter," said Bardo. "And since the DK's botched their first attempt and lost a key man in the second, I don't think they'll return to your home."

"If you know who these people are, why can't you just arrest them," asked John.

"I wish we could," said Bardo. "We need more evidence. We're working hard on the case and will keep you informed. Ms. Herrera, I'll need to get Mr. Taylor's address from you. I'm going to place an unmarked deputy there for 24 hours and order regular patrols after that."

Di wrote Jason's address in Bardo's notebook as he stood to leave.

"You all have my card. Call me if you think of anything else."

"We will. Thank you, lieutenant," said Di.

CHAPTER 26

After Di left for the hospital after the meeting at Reina's, Jason went inside and looked up Andru Mixon's number in the school directory. Andru was the makeup artist for the Florida IT theatre department that Jason had told the others about.

"Andru, this is Jason Taylor from the journalism department. How are you?"

"Jason Taylor. To what do I owe the honor of this phone call?"

"Well Andru, some friends and I have been invited to a costume party in a few days and I was wondering if we could hire you to make us up. We want to look like real people but be unrecognizable as ourselves."

"You came to the right man, Jason. I would love to make you and your friends up. When is your soiree?"

"The exact date hasn't been set yet. Probably some night this coming week. I can let you know as soon as I know. I wanted to check with you first to see if you would be available."

"Anytime this week after school would work fine. We're in between shows right now. Have you heard? We're doing South Pacific next."

"That's a classic show, Andru. I'm sure it will be a smash. When the time comes, do you think you could come to my place in Cooper City to do us?"

"I would be honored, Jason. And don't worry, I'll bring my full bag of tricks. I have a huge collection of prosthetics I've been dying to try out."

"You're the best, Andru. I'll get back to you as soon as I know the date."

Jason next phoned Tommy. He had to confirm that his friend was really on board with this operation.

"Tommy, Jason. I just spoke with my disguise master. He's available to come over to my place any time this week to make us up. Are you sure you really want to be involved in this?"

"Hell yes, Jason. Do you know how boring it is just sitting in your car watching and taking pictures of people? I'm ready for some action. I already talked to Hector and Joe. They want in, too."

"Do you think four of us will be enough?" Jason asked.

"Should be. The dark blue windbreakers I have are just like the ones the DHS and ICE agents wear, but they just say AGENT on the back. So, they shouldn't be able to get us on impersonating law enforcement since my guys and I are all agents, in the occupational sense. I'll put you on my payroll for this case so the same will apply to you."

"I'm thinking we show up between ten and eleven p.m. so that Rebecca Cross is still there," said Jason. "I just read an article that said it is common procedure for DHS to show up for surprise inspections at these detention camps. If we all show up in your jackets and demand entry in order to conduct an unannounced inspection, they should take us for Homeland Security, their bosses, and let us in. Once inside, I'll show the photo of the van, kids and Victor to Cross. I'll then tell her we are doing a complete transfer of the children to another facility and, if she doesn't want to spend the next twenty-five years in prison as a human trafficker she will instruct her staff to assist us."

"So, all we need then is for the priest's buses to pull up on time," said Tommy.

"Right. And we need the ACLU guy to give us some assurances that this was legally justifiable if it comes to that," said Jason. "The availability of the buses will determine what night we do this."

"And, we need confirmation that they have enough distributors with vehicles to meet the buses," added Tommy.

"I'll text Father Pat to see how he's doing and ask if he can arrange for us to use the parking lot of a church in the area to do the transferring," said Jason.

Fifteen minutes later, Jason received Father Pat's reply. He had secured the use of two full-size church buses so far, and was hearing from many in his network who were volunteering to meet the buses with their own vans and cars to distribute the children to safe houses and church sanctuaries. Some would be driving many hours, from northern and central Florida, to help. He was hoping all would be ready to go by Tuesday.

CHAPTER 27

Lt. Bardo was pleased when he learned that Miami-Dade had assigned a different detective, Lt. Frank Morrison, to accompany him when he visited Rico Valbuena at three that afternoon. He didn't know Morrison, but anyone would have been better than that Escobar they gave him last night. He was still angry that she hadn't told him that Victor's uncle, Rico, lived next door when they were there. On the other hand, he had learned more since last night so this should be a more fruitful interview. "Don't question fate," he told himself.

He and Morrison met at an Allapattah convenience store before driving their own cars to the fourplex. Morrison was an all-business type of detective, probably in his fifties. He reminded Bardo of a commander he had in the marines … right down to the jar head haircut. He seemed to know a lot about Rico and the Dominican Kings. He told Bardo his suspicion that the DK's may have expanded their operations into human trafficking didn't surprise him at all.

Pulling up to the fourplex, Bardo wished he had asked Escobar if "next door" meant the unit next to Maria's or the building next door. They would try the next-door unit first. The iron gate out front was unlocked. Carlotta answered the door.

"I'm Lieutenant Bardo from Broward County and this is Lieutenant Morrison from Miami-Dade," said Bardo through the screen door, as they both showed their badges. "We would like to talk to Ricardo Valbuena."

"Rico," hollered Carlotta back into the unit.

They watched Rico walk slowly through the unit toward the front door, scratching his balls through his baggy black sweat pants. He looked like he had just gotten up.

"Sorry to interrupt your beauty sleep, Ricardo," said Morrison. "Lieutenant Bardo here from Broward County has a few questions for you. Do you mind if we come in?"

"I don't let no cops into my house if I don't have to," said Rico, opening the screen door, stepping out front and squinting in the bright sunlight. "What you bothering me for?"

"Why did your nephew, Victor, and two of your other gang members try to kill the occupants of a home in Dania Beach yesterday?" asked Bardo.

"My nephew, may he go to hell, was crazy … and stupid. Sounds like you know more about this than I do. You tell me."

"I think Victor was trafficking immigrant kids out of the Everglades Detention Facility," said Bardo.

"So, they showed you the picture."

Bardo hesitated for just a split second. "Yeah, they showed me the picture," he bluffed. "Now I want you to tell me more about it."

"I don't know anything about it."

"Then, who showed you the picture?" asked Bardo.

Rico leaned in toward Bardo, looking him in the eye. "You're fucking with me. You didn't see no picture. Nice try, cop."

Two DK's had walked up to the screen door from inside the unit and were looking out at them. One was noticeably shorter than the other. Bardo made note.

"Why don't you introduce us to your friends, Rico?" asked Bardo.

"Those are my babysitters. My wife and I are going out to a movie."

Bardo stepped to the screen door. "What's your name?" he asked the shorter one.

"Christopher Columbus," he answered.

"Watch your mouth, hombrecito," said Morrison. "The lieutenant asked you a question."

"We call him el enano," said Rico.

"The dwarf," Morrison translated for Bardo. Miami-Dade County requires all of their law enforcement officers to be able to speak Spanish since more than half of the county's 2.8 million residents are Spanish speakers.

"Step outside," Bardo ordered.

The little one didn't move.

"Do it," ordered Rico, relieved that the focus was no longer on him.

He stepped outside. The other DK remained behind the screen door.

"Let's see your ID," ordered Bardo.

El enano reached into the front pocket of his brown cargo shorts and pulled out a Florida driver's license and handed it to Bardo.

Oscar Domingo Ruiz Santiago, it read. It listed his height as five feet.

"Oscar," said Bardo, "I need you to come in to my office with me and answer a few questions."

"Am I under arrest, chief?"

"No. In fact, we'll pay for an Uber ride home for you."

"You better go, enano," said Rico.

Bardo, Oscar and Morrison turned and started walking back to their cars. After a few steps Bardo said, "wait here for a second," and walked back to Rico, who was still standing outside his front door. "One more thing," Bardo said. "Who is Manuel?"

"I don't know no Manuel," answered Rico.

"What is Victor's cousin's name?" Bardo asked.

"I'm not going to answer any more of your questions without my lawyer present," Rico told him.

"That's your right," Bardo told him. "You might want to ask yourself why I'm interested, though. We'll talk again, I'm sure, Rico."

Back at the Broward Sheriff's Dania Beach office, Bardo walked Oscar into the building and put him in an interview room. He then went to his desk and looked up Oscar's record which said he was twenty-one years old. He had already been arrested nine times and had spent eighteen months in juvenile detention.

None of Oscar's Miami-Dade mugshots looked much like him now, though. He now had a shaved head and an attempt at a goatee. He also had the Dominican flag tattooed on the top of his head and various gang symbols adorning his neck.

He had Oscar come out into the hallway and a deputy took a photo of him. Bardo wanted to later show the Herrera's a photo lineup that included Oscar.

Oscar hadn't spoken on the way there but now, back in the interview room, he wanted to know what Bardo wanted with him.

"You're a person of interest in the attempted murder of a couple in Dania Beach yesterday," Bardo told him. "Why didn't you go back with Victor when he went to their house a second time?"

"I don't know what you're talking about," said Oscar. "I was hanging out in Allapattah all day yesterday."

A deputy stuck her head in and called Bardo out into the hall where she told him that a judge had just issued a search warrant for Victor's unit. Miami-Dade had scheduled the search for one hour from now. That left Bardo only about twenty more minutes to work on Oscar. He went back in and sat down.

"We'll be conducting a search of Victor's apartment in about one hour, so you'll be riding back with me. What do you think your gang buddies will think when they see you show up with a bunch of cops who will do a very thorough and lengthy search of Victor's place? After we get out of the car I'll make a point to thank you for the excellent information you've given us."

"You think my bro's will believe your bullshit?" Oscar asked.

"Yeah, I think they will. You can't see that those guys don't respect you ... don't even like you? They call you el enano. You probably won't even be around next week, once I get more evidence and we come back to arrest you."

Oscar was silent.

"We have Victor's phone and know that he called you about an hour before the shooting. You've got to start looking out for yourself, Oscar. Tell me who the third shooter was yesterday and why you went to the Herrera's house, and be prepared to testify honestly and you'll be looking at two or three years instead of twenty-five to thirty. You've got your whole life ahead of you. Do you really want to rot in a shitty Florida penitentiary until you're nearly fifty?"

"You know the Herrera's both survived your murder attempt," he continued. "They know what you look like and are both in the hospital waiting to pick you out of a photo lineup."

Bardo could tell Oscar was thinking. He still was silent, though.

Finally, "If I snitch to you I'm a dead man."

Excellent, thought Bardo. The little shit all but admitted to his involvement.

"And you think by leading a search party back to the Valbuena's they're going to throw a fiesta for you? You're in a tough spot, Oscar, and I'm the best friend you have right now. Tell me the truth about what happened yesterday and I'll see that you get a private cell ... with your own TV. You won't have any contact with the general population."

Oscar knew he didn't want to ride back to Rico's with the cops. Nor did he want to snitch.

"Okay, give me the private cell and I'll tell you what you want to know when you get back."

Bardo knew that Oscar was more afraid of showing up at Rico's with a bunch of cops than he was of being locked up. He also knew that Oscar would clam up and give him nothing once he got back.

Bardo stood. "I have to make the arrangements. I'll be right back."

The department's computer tech had prepared a digital photo lineup that included Oscar and five other similar looking young Hispanic men. Bardo asked her to print out two color copies for showing to the Herrera's later. It was time to go. He went back to the interview room.

"You know what? All of the private cells are occupied. My bad for not checking first." Bardo looked at his watch. "It's time to go. Looks like you can sleep on your own mattress or couch or whatever tonight."

Oscar stood up. "You cops are always fucking with people, aren't you? I was just going to make up some bullshit to tell you anyway."

Bardo timed his drive so he arrived back at the fourplex at exactly four. The Miami-Dade vehicles pulled up at the same time. Lt. Morrison was heading their team. Bardo got out and greeted him before letting Oscar out of the back seat.

"Thanks, Oscar. The Broward County Sheriff appreciates your cooperation," Bardo called to him as Oscar walked to Rico's door.

Rico had anticipated the search warrant and had gone through Victor's unit that morning with Maria, removing all weapons, drugs and drug paraphernalia.

As a result, the search turned up nothing of value for Bardo's case. He walked over to Rico's door before leaving and knocked. Rico answered. "Now what?"

Bardo looked through the screen door and saw Oscar sitting in a chair in the middle of the room.

"Oscar," he called through the screen door. "Are you sure you don't want to come back with me?"

"*Vete a la mierda, policía*," Oscar replied.

Bardo knew a fuck you when he heard it, even in Spanish.

"Have it your way, enano. *Buena suerte.*"

Bardo heard the inside door slam as he walked to his car. He would go to All Souls Hospital to show the photo lineup to the Herrera's. He hoped Oscar would still be alive to arrest if they ID'd him.

CHAPTER 28

At first Antonio thought he was dreaming. "Unh, unh, unh," he heard, along with a higher pitched, "Ahw, ahw, ahw."

He sat up, looked around and saw an older boy hunched over the back of a smaller boy who was bent over one of the benches along the perimeter of their cage.

"*Oh dios mio!*" he thought. He threw off his foil blanket, got up, leaped over sleeping boys, grabbed the older boy by his hair and violently pulled him backwards to the floor. The older boy's pants were down around his ankles which made it hard for him to quickly get back up. Antonio lifted his foot and stomped down hard between the boy's legs. The boy doubled up and began moaning loudly.

Antonio then turned his attention to the five- or six-year-old victim. "It's alright now, *pequeñin*. You'll be okay, I promise."

The boy pulled his pants up and Antonio knelt down next to the writhing older boy as if to ask if he was okay. Instead Antonio punched him as hard as he could in the side of his face.

The guards in the control room had seen and heard what happened and two of them had run to the cage gate, unlocked it and were running toward Antonio.

"You know the rule about no fighting, paco," said the first guard to reach him, as he slapped Antonio hard upside his face. The other guard grabbed Antonio's wrists and cuffed him behind his back.

They looked down at the doubled-up boy on the floor. "Looks like these faggot wetbacks are at it again," said one.

"Get up, faggot boy," said the other guard as he pulled him to his feet. He quickly cuffed the older boy, Jose Cordova, a fourteen-year-old from Mexico.

Cordova's pants were still around his ankles and he was still moaning as the guards held him upright by each arm.

"Looks like you got a little mud on the helmet there, paco," said one of the guards.

"The little faggot needs to get hosed off," said the other.

The two guards dragged Cordova out the cage gate, telling Antonio to walk ahead of them, and headed to the shower room.

"Looks like this one wanted to go first," said one of the guards, referring to Antonio. "And then got pissed off when all he was going to get was sloppy seconds."

They got to the shower room and pushed Cordova, his hands still cuffed behind his back, toward the far wall. He stumbled and fell as one of the guards uncoiled a thick hose from the wall and turned it on full. Cordova doubled up, trying to protect himself from the powerful stream of water.

"Straighten him out, Carl," said the guard with the hose. "We gotta make sure his *cojones* are clean."

Carl went over, grabbed Cordova by the upper arms and lifted him up. "Hey, watch where you aim that," he said to the guard with the hose. "I don't want to get wetback jizz and shit on me."

When the hosing was finally finished, Carl let Cordova go and he crumpled to the floor.

The guard who did the hosing grabbed Antonio by the arm. "I'm taking this one to his new room. I'll be right back to help you with Casanova."

"This still isn't as bad as the gangs and the police back home," Antonio kept telling himself as he was led down the hall to an isolation room where his cuffs were removed and he was shoved in.

The guard returned to the shower room and helped Carl drag Cordova to another isolation room where they removed his cuffs before Carl put a boot to his bare ass, kicking Cordova across the small room.

CHAPTER 29

"So, you brought your new friends back with you, enano," said Rico as Oscar entered. The shades were pulled and Oscar's eyes had to adjust after coming in from the bright sunlight. Rico was sitting in a large overstuffed chair toward the back of the living room. Two other DK's were slouched on a sagging sofa to Rico's right. One of them, Enrique, was cleaning his fingernails with a black, eleven-inch, full tang tactical knife. The other, Benny, was playing Frontline Commando on his phone.

"I told those cops nothing, Rico," said Oscar. "It was because of Victor they got the search warrant."

"But it wasn't my dead nephew talking to the cops today, it was you."

"I swear on my mother, Rico, I told them nothing. You are my family. I would never betray my family."

"Have a seat, enano," said Rico, motioning to a straight-back wood chair in the middle of the floor. "We will wait for their search to be done. They won't find anything."

"*Carlotta, traednos algunas cervezas,*" Rico called out. Carlotta quickly appeared and handed out four cans of Presidente, the most popular Dominican beer in Little Santo Domingo.

"So, what did you and your lieutenant friend talk about?" Rico asked after taking a long pull on his Presidente. "You're not locked up, so he must have liked what you had to say."

"I'm not locked up because I told him nothing, and he had nothing on me. That's the whole story. I hate cops as much as you do, so I wish you would quit calling him my friend."

"I'm just fucking with you, enano. I know you wouldn't say anything."

"Hey, it's been a long day, Rico, you know?" said Oscar. "Do you mind if I go home for a while? I can come back later if you need me."

"Not at all, Oscar," said Rico, using his given name for the first time. "Enrique will walk you to the back door."

Enrique had since put his knife back in his belt sheath. He got up the same time Oscar did. Oscar was well aware of gang hierarchy and protocol. It was totally normal for a junior member to be escorted when walking through a captain's home. He walked ahead of Enrique down the narrow hallway.

At the moment he reached the back door, Enrique wrapped his left hand around Oscar's forehead and plunged his tactical knife upward through Oscar's neck and into his brain. Oscar was killed instantly. Enrique admired his raised right bicep as he held Oscar's body upright by his knife handle.

Enrique had been taught this effective method of killing by Rico, who preferred it because death was instant and little blood was spilled. However, because it required close proximity directly behind the victim, as well as complete surprise, the opportunity to use it was rare.

"Benny," Enrique yelled down the hall, "I'm ready for you."

As Benny neared the doorway to the kitchen on his way to the back door, Enrique added, "Grab a couple of big trash bags from the kitchen."

"They're under the sink," Rico called from the living room.

Benny arrived at the back door with two 65-gallon, heavy-duty black trash bags.

Enrique told him he was going to lift Oscar up and, when he did, he wanted Benny to put one of the bags under Oscar's feet and pull it up as far as it would go. Enrique started lifting Oscar using the still-embedded knife, but it simply started slicing through Oscar's head. So, he pulled his knife out and lifted Oscar from under his arms. Because the trash bag was so big and Oscar so small Benny was able to pull it up to Oscar's shoulders.

"Hold him up," said Enrique, and he lowered the other bag over Oscar's head. It came down almost to his ankles. The two then laid Oscar down in the hallway, tightened and tied off the bag cinches and returned to the living room.

"Where do you want us to take him, Rico?" asked Enrique.

"Put on gloves and wipe down every inch of those bags," said Rico. "Once its dark put him on the floor in your back seat. At three this morning take him to North River Drive at 32nd and throw him over the concrete wall next to the railroad tracks. There are no cameras there."

CHAPTER 30

A ll three occupants in John and Robin Herrera's hospital room were lightly napping when Lt. Bardo came calling with his photo lineups. Di, in a corner chair, was the first to stir.

"Lieutenant," she said, after opening her eyes to see Bardo standing in the room's entrance. "Come in. What can we do for you?"

"I have a photo lineup I'd like your parents to look at when they're able." He took the two 8x10 color printouts from an envelope.

Just then John, already in a sitting-up position, opened his eyes. "Lieutenant, I'm impressed with your work ethic; six o'clock on a Saturday and you're still working."

"That's the job, Mr. Herrera. I'm looking forward to a family day tomorrow." Bardo walked over to his bed and handed John one of the lineups. "Do you recognize any of these as one of the people that shot you?"

Using his uninjured arm, John picked up his reading glasses from the tray suspended over his lap, put them on, then took the lineup from Bardo. After examining it he pointed to Oscar, saying, "There's something about this one. I couldn't swear to it, though. They were wearing bandanas. Robin, wake up. The lieutenant's here with some mug shots to look at."

Mrs. Herrera opened her eyes, then blinked a few times. "Hello, lieutenant."

Di took the second lineup from Bardo, walked around to the side of her mom's bed and gave her some water before showing her the photos. "Mom, Lt. Bardo wants to know if you recognize any of these guys as one of the shooters." Di held the photo as Robin studied it. Her gaze stopped on the second photo from the left in the top row and the shooting replayed, horribly, in her mind.

She couldn't lift her arms, but said to Di, "That's one of them. He was looking right at me. Top row, second from the left." It was Oscar's picture.

"Are you sure, Mrs. Herrera?" asked Bardo. "You and your husband have said they were wearing bandanas and wrap-around sun glasses."

"Its that stupid tattoo on his head. I recognize that," she said.

Bardo collected his lineup photos from the Herreras, thanked them and wished them a speedy recovery, and went out into the hall to phone Lt. Morrison.

"Frank, it's Grady Bardo. My shooting victims just gave me a positive ID on Oscar Santiago, the little DK I took in for questioning. I'm heading over to arrest him. Are you available to help?"

"Hi Grady. I'm in. What time do you want to meet at Rico's?"

"I should be able to get there by seven," said Bardo.

"That works for me," said Morrison. "I'll let the Miami

PD know what we're up to in case we need backup. I'll see you there."

Rico knew it wouldn't be dark for another couple of hours. He was getting nervous about keeping Oscar in his home for that long.

Enrique and Benny were on the couch watching a soccer match.

"Enrique," said Rico, "I've changed my mind. Take Oscar out now and put him in your trunk."

Enrique was strong enough to carry Oscar's body, wrapped in the trash bags, under one arm. He took him out to his '82 Olds eighty-eight sedan parked on the street, unlocked his trunk with his free hand and laid Oscar inside.

Bardo and Morrison pulled up fifteen minutes later and, as is procedure for this type of situation, parked their vehicles so as to box in the car out front. Bardo got out of his car and walked up to Morrison, who was still in his vehicle and had his radio mic in his hand. He lowered his window.

"I've got a feeling about this," he said to Bardo. "I'm calling Miami PD to see if they can get a cadaver dog over here, along with a couple of backup units."

When he was done, he and Bardo walked through the unlocked iron gate and up to Rico's door. Rico had raised the shade on his front window after the Oscar business was finished and saw the two approaching.

"El enano left here an hour ago," Rico quickly said to Enrique and Benny. "He didn't say where he was going." He then went to his front door to meet the two detectives.

He opened his inside door and said through the screen, "You two move into the neighborhood? You're over here enough."

"We're here for Oscar Santiago," said Bardo. "Send him out."

"Oscar left about an hour ago," said Rico.

Just then a Miami PD car pulled up in front. They had no dog, but two uniformed officers got out and walked up to the door, backing up Bardo and Morrison.

"We need to come in and look around," said Morrison.

"Not without a warrant you don't," responded Rico.

"We don't need a warrant," said Bardo, "we're pursuing an attempted murder suspect who has been positively identified by his two victims and he was last seen walking into your home. Are you going to let us in or are we going to have to arrest you, too?"

"Why didn't you say so," said Rico, opening the screen door. "Can I get you guys a Presidente?" asked Rico, holding up his can. "It's the finest Dominican beer."

"Never mind the beer," said Bardo, "What's down there?" he asked, looking down the hallway.

"The usual," said Rico, "a kitchen, a shitter, Carlotta in the bedroom with her iPad."

"Come on in, guys," Morrison said to the two officers at the door. "Keep an eye on these two," motioning to Enrique and Benny.

The two detectives headed down the hallway. In the kitchen they made note of the box of sixty-five-gallon trash bags still on the counter. They checked the closet and under the bed in the bedroom. At the back door they noticed what looked like small blood drops on the dirty grout between the floor tiles. Morrison called his office and told them to send an evidence processing team, then they walked back to the living room.

"You been doing yard work, Rico?" Bardo asked.

"Why?"

"You've got a box of yard-waste size trash bags on your kitchen counter," said Bardo. "What did you get rid of?"

"Those are Carlotta's. She likes to work in the yard. Always trimming and weeding."

"Stand up," Morrison ordered Benny and Enrique.

Enrique's tactical knife was in its sheath attached to his belt. "Take off your belt and put it on the table," Morrison told him.

There was a coffee table in front of the couch. Enrique removed his belt and put it on the table. Bardo picked it up, removed the knife with his latex-gloved hands and carefully examined it. He saw a small speck of what could be blood where the blade met the handle. He took a plastic evidence bag from his pocket, took the knife and sheath off the belt and put them inside the bag.

"Let's see some ID," Bardo told Enrique.

"I don't have an ID with me," said Enrique. "I need an ID to sit in my friend's home and watch futbol?"

Just then, they all heard loud barking from outside. They looked out the front window. The cadaver dog unit had arrived and the dog was barking and pawing at the trunk of the Olds 88.

"Whose car is that?" asked Morrison.

"I don't know," said Rico. "It's been out there all day."

Morrison pulled out his cuffs and nodded to the two officers. Morrison cuffed Rico and the officers cuffed Enrique and Benny.

"Carlotta, call the lawyer," Rico yelled down the hall.

The officer who was patting down Enrique felt car keys in his front pocket and pulled them out.

"What do you want to bet that these keys are going to fit the trunk of that car?" said Morrison to Bardo.

"What do you want to bet that dog is smelling little Oscar?" Bardo responded.

The detectives ordered the DK's outside and Morrison walked to the back of the car with the keys. He handed them to the dog's handler, Sgt. Heccheveria.

"You brought the dog, sergeant. You get to open the trunk."

Heccheveria found the right key, ordered his dog to sit, opened the trunk and they all looked in at the bundle inside wrapped in black trash bags.

The evidence unit had just arrived and Morrison called over to them to call for the coroner. He and Bardo didn't need to look inside to know it was Oscar.

Since they were in Miami-Dade county, Morrison was the one to inform Rico, Benny and Enrique that they were under arrest on suspicion of murder and read them their rights.

"Put them in separate cars," Morrison told the uniformed Miami PD officers who were removing the contents of the DK's pockets and bagging them.

The police photographer was taking photos of the open trunk, Oscar inside the now-opened trash bags, the car and the DK's before going into the unit.

On his drive back to Broward County, Bardo was thinking about how two of the Herrera shooters were now dead. One of the two DK's at Rico's was probably the third shooter. He had tried to tell Oscar not to go back there. There was still the matter of the motive: the suspected trafficking of immigrant children from the Everglades facility. And Rebecca Cross's obvious involvement. That could wait. Tomorrow would be Sunday. Maybe he would finally get that family day.

CHAPTER 31

I t was nearly seven by the time Di got back to Jason's from the hospital. He had given her a key and when she let herself in the front door she found him on the couch just waking up and the Miami Marlins post-game show on the TV.

She had eaten next to nothing while at the hospital and had stopped at Panera Bread on her way home and picked up food for both of them.

"Hey there professor, I hope you're hungry. I picked up some sandwiches on my way here."

Jason got up and joined her in the kitchen where they hugged and she gave him a kiss.

"So, did you miss me?" she asked.

"Actually, yes, I did."

"What do you mean, *actually*? That surprised you?"

"Yeah, it surprised me. I haven't missed someone for a long time. Tell the truth, aren't *you* a bit surprised by all that's happened?"

"I'm just fucking with you, Professor Taylor," she said, drawing out *Professor Taylor* as she pinched the front of his tee shirt and pulled him toward her. "Of course I'm surprised," she said softly, her green eyes almost sparkling. She pressed her soft lips to his as he wrapped his arms around her and returned her kiss. Jason's thought was that he could almost feel his heart melting. Their lips parted and they looked into each other's eyes, not speaking. Di had never felt as safe as she did now in Jason's strong embrace. Jason stroked Di's long, dark hair, gently pushing a strand away from her cheek.

"Do you think the sandwiches will wait?" said Jason.

"I think they'll wait," said Di, as Jason took her hand and led her to his bedroom.

Forty-five minutes later they were back in the kitchen. Di was barefoot, wearing one of Jason's long white tee shirts, had put her hair in a ponytail and was taking their food out of the bag when her phone rang. It was Lt. Bardo calling to tell her that the individual that her parents had identified had been murdered by his fellow gang members and that Victor's uncle, Rico, had been arrested, along with two other DK's. Bardo was fairly confident that one of those two was the third shooter at her parents' home.

"Does that mean that I'm safe now?" she asked. "And Reina and Tomas?"

"You should be," replied Bardo. "I don't think any of the other Dominican Kings will take up Victor and Rico's vendetta since it doesn't affect them."

"And what about your suspicion of trafficking out of Everglades?" Di asked.

"Well, we don't have any actionable evidence yet, but we're monitoring Rebecca Cross's cell phone. We'll see what comes of that."

Di thanked him for all his hard work on their behalf and Bardo assured her he would remain in contact.

Jason had taken two beers out of his fridge and was opening them. "What did he say?" he asked after Di hung up.

"The DK's killed the one that my mom and dad identified when Bardo showed them some photos today. Bardo and the Miami-Dade cops found his body in a trunk and arrested the uncle of the one you shot and two others. He thinks one of them was the third shooter yesterday."

"Wow, that guy works fast."

"I'm glad he did," said Di. "I feel a lot safer ... not that I didn't feel safe with you anyway ... also. You know what I mean."

"I know that I'm ready for one of those sandwiches."

Di handed him his, saying, "We have to move fast, too." They sat down at Jason's small kitchen table. "Did you learn anything more today about our plan?"

"Yeah. I talked with Andru, the makeup guy from the drama department. He's excited about disguising the four of us. I told him it was for a costume party. He said he's going to use prosthetics. Should be interesting."

"I can't wait to see how you'll look."

"I talked to Tommy. He and Hector and Joe are on board. Father Pat texted me that he has two buses arranged and he's confident that he can get two more. And he has a lot of people volunteering to meet the buses, take some kids, and shelter them. He thinks they will be ready to go by Tuesday night."

"I'll call Reina after we eat and see if she's heard anything more from Jeffries at the ACLU. My god, this actually could happen."

Di's phone rang just as she was finishing her sandwich. "It's Reina," she told Jason, "we must be on the same wavelength."

"Reina, hi, I was just going to call you. How did your showing go?"

"Oh Di, it went great. The arts editor for the Palm Beach Post was there with a photographer. They're going to do an article about my work for next Sunday's paper."

"Wow, congratulations. I'm so happy for you. I know you've been super busy, but I was wondering if Jim Jeffries had gotten back to you."

"I just got off the phone with him. That's why I'm calling. He had to run this by the ACLU's national board to get guidance on this."

"And?"

"He emailed all of them a description of the situation here. Since it's the weekend not all of them have responded yet, but the ones that have are in agreement that this could be a precedent-setting case if there *is* any prosecution. If we can provide them with evidence of the abuse, suicides and human trafficking at Everglades there is a very good chance that the ACLU will provide full legal representation for anyone who may be charged in the rescue. He'll be able to tell us more on Monday, after he's heard back from the full board."

"More great news! I can't wait to tell Jason. I have some news for you, too."

"Tell me."

"The police detective investigating the shooting showed my mom and dad a photo lineup earlier today in the hospital and they picked out one of the shooters. The detective went over to Allapattah to bring him in and his gang had murdered him."

"Oh my god."

"His body was in a car trunk out in front of their place. They arrested three gang members there. He thinks one of them is the third shooter."

"I hope that means you're safe now. How *are* your parents?"

"They think my dad can go home tomorrow. My mom might still be in for another week … Reina, Jason's going to throw something at me if I don't get off and tell him your news."

The two said goodbye and Di shared what she had been told about the ACLU *and* Reina's show.

Jason was finishing off his beer when Di asked him, "what do *we* do now?"

"What do you want to do?"

"I asked you first," she said, smiling.

"I know I don't want you to leave," he said.

"And I want to stay. I just don't know if that's the right thing to do. We were kind of thrown together here by circumstance."

Jason reached across the table and took her hand. "I think sometimes things happen for a reason. Right now, I can't imagine you not being here."

"But things have happened so quickly. Whatever it is we have hasn't been tested."

"Hasn't been tested?" Jason's eyes grew wide. "What do you call what's happened over the past three days? I think it would be more accurate to say that what we have has been forged in fire."

"You're right," Di said. "Damn it, Jason Taylor, you're right. I just remembered something you used to say in class … you told us, *'be here now'*; if your focus is totally in the present you are best able to understand and report accurately on what is happening. Well, I like what is happening in the present. I feel like we're partners. How about you?"

"Absolutely, one-hundred percent," said Jason. "I like what's happening in the present, too … and I hope what's happening continues for a long time."

"I'm glad we got that settled," said Di, squeezing Jason's hand and finishing off her beer. "I definitely have to get more of my clothes tomorrow."

CHAPTER 32

By Sunday morning Rebecca Cross was beside herself with worry and fear. She sat at her kitchen table in her kimono, drinking coffee and running her hand over her short brown hair. She felt certain that Lt. Bardo would be banging on her front door at any moment with a warrant for her arrest or a demand that she come in for questioning. She took an Ativan, taken from the camp's dispensary, to calm down.

She had come up with a story if she needed one: she believed that the children being picked up were going to be reunited with their family member, just like the children did. Captain Lopez was the trafficker's inside person. She may have been guilty of being trusting and gullible, but that was all. Lopez would accuse her, but it would be her word against his now that Victor was dead.

Her bosses at DCA turn a blind eye to most of what goes on at the facility, but this would be different. Multiple federal agencies now had task forces investigating human trafficking. If she was arrested she would have to sell her townhouse to pay for a lawyer.

She opened her laptop and Googled which countries have no extradition treaties with the U.S. She found that most of them were in Africa. But there was one – the Federated States of Micronesia – that caught her eye. It looked like a tropical paradise in the middle of the Pacific Ocean.

She checked flights and found she could fly there one-way for fourteen hundred dollars if she left on Wednesday. The damn flight had eighteen- and seventeen-hour layovers in San Francisco and Honolulu. She would have to hope that an arrest warrant wasn't issued for her before she deplaned in Micronesia. Fortunately, her passport was current. She could list her townhouse with a realtor and they could transfer the proceeds of the sale to her in Micronesia. Maybe she would find a nice Polynesian girlfriend there and settle down.

Rebecca knew she would need more money, though. The only way she could think to get money quick was to sell another load of kids tomorrow or Tuesday. She had been monitoring local news online and had read that Victor's uncle and two others had been arrested at the same building in Allapattah where she had dropped off Victor and his cousin ... but they had been arrested on suspicion of murder, not trafficking.

They were her only contacts for selling the kids. Maybe, she thought, she should try calling the other number she had reached Victor on ... the one that a woman had answered. She was probably Victor's girlfriend and might be able to connect her with someone who would want to pick up where Victor left off. But she couldn't have her phone number showing up on the girlfriend's phone a second time. The job-seeking cousin story wouldn't work to explain that.

Then she remembered hearing about Burner phones when she worked at the adult prison in the Panhandle. She researched it and discovered that Burner was an app she could download to her phone that would give her a second number that would show up when she called someone. So, she downloaded the app and called Maria using her new Burner number.

"Hola," answered Maria.

"Hi, this is Victor's friend that called the other day. I heard about Victor. I'm so sorry."

"Well, then you know that Victor's not here. Why are you calling me?"

"I have ten more kids that I want to place with whoever Victor was getting them for. I was hoping you could help me."

With Victor gone, Maria now had no source of support for herself and her baby. If she could get Rico's van and keys, she thought, maybe she could make the pickup and make some money. But first she would have to get the money to pay Cross. She would have to see if Carlotta knew who Rico was selling the kids to. Maybe they would front her the money for a new load.

"I will have to see if it's possible," said Maria. "If it is, I'll call you back."

"It would have to happen either tomorrow or Tuesday," Rebecca told her.

"I'll call you back if I can do it," said Maria, and hung up.

Maria went next door to Carlotta's and told her about the phone call.

"I don't know who Rico was selling the kids to," Carlotta told her.

Miguel was lying on the couch. He had been gone the day before and missed what had happened with Oscar and the arrests.

"Miguel, who was Rico selling the kids to?" Carlotta asked him.

"I'm pretty sure it was Carlos Salazar over on twenty-seventh street."

"Do you know where the van and the keys are?" she asked.

"I think papa left them with Carlos, too."

"Do you know Carlos?" Maria asked Carlotta. "Do you want to help me with this? We can split whatever we make."

"I'll think about it," said Carlotta. "I do need more money for Rico's lawyer. I know Carlos. Let's walk over there and talk to him. Miguel, go over to Maria's and watch Eddie while we're gone."

When Carlotta and Maria got to Carlos's house, he and two other DK's were sitting out front.

Carlos recognized Carlotta. "Carlotta, did you come to visit me? Come in."

Carlotta opened the white iron gate and she and Maria walked up to the three men.

"I heard about Rico," said Carlos. "That's too bad. Oscar wasn't worth going to jail for. Who is your friend?"

"This is Maria, Victor's girlfriend."

"Maria, I'm sorry about Victor. He was too good to die so young. What can I do for you ladies?"

"Maria got a phone call that there is another load of kids that can be picked up if it is done tomorrow or Tuesday. We were thinking that if we had the van and the payment we could make the pickup."

"Ah, that didn't go so well last week when Victor tried it," said Carlos.

"I'll tell them the pickup has to be at the front entrance," said Maria. "Victor told me they made their pickup at the back entrance and that is how they got in trouble. If you approve, we would do it on Tuesday night."

"Well, the van is out back," said Carlos. "I have the keys and the money that Victor gave back to Rico. You two really want to do this?"

Maria nudged Carlotta. "How much would we make?" asked Carlotta.

"Fifteen hundred," replied Carlos. "Come back on Tuesday when you're ready to go and I'll give you the van and the money. I hope it works out better for you than it did for Victor. You bring them back here when you're done and I'll pay you then."

"Thank you, Carlos," said Carlotta. "You won't be sorry. Maria and I will be back on Tuesday night."

"Thank you, Carlos," said Maria.

On the walk back home, Maria called Cross. "We can make the pickup on Tuesday night. No back door this time, though. The pickup will have to be at the front entrance."

Cross didn't like the front entrance pickup, but she needed the money and she wouldn't be coming back to Everglades after Tuesday anyway.

"That will work. Be there at exactly eleven p.m."

She gave Maria the address of Everglades and directions to get there and told her to make sure she had the entire three thousand.

Rebecca got back online and made her reservation to fly to Pohnpei, Micronesia on Wednesday. She then looked up car dealers near Miami International. She would sell her car to one of them on her way to the airport.

CHAPTER 33

———

Father Pat had finished saying his masses for the day and was back in his rectory office. He had many phone messages and emails to respond to about picking up and housing the children on Tuesday night. His secretary was assisting him in recording the names and addresses of each shelter volunteer.

Jim Jeffries had told him it was important that each child be documented, along with where and with whom each child would be staying. The ACLU needed to show that they wanted to work *with* Homeland Security rather than against them.

There would be two Spanish-speaking volunteers on each of the four buses who would record the children's names, origins, the family members they crossed the border with, and names and contact information for any relatives they may have living in the U.S.

The collecting of this information had to be completed before the children were assigned to the shelter volunteers. Their records would also show which children went with which volunteers. All volunteers were being vetted through their parish priests.

Father Ernesto, the pastor of St. Stephens, a large parish in Weston that was just twelve miles from the Everglades facility, had volunteered their parking lot to be the staging area for the transfer of the children to the volunteers.

With an average of four children going with each volunteer, that meant that there would be approximately forty volunteer vehicles, in addition to the four buses.

The buses and their on-board information gatherers were to meet at St. Stephens at ten pm. Di would be an on-board volunteer on the bus that was to arrive first at Everglades. Father Pat had agreed to be the other volunteer on that bus in the belief that a priest's presence would have a calming effect on the children.

Two of the buses would be full-size school buses and the other two were Prevost 55-passenger motor coaches. It had been agreed that the motor coaches would be the first to load at Everglades since they most resembled the charter buses that DHS uses to transport large numbers of detainees.

The plan was for Tommy, Jason, Hector and Joe to arrive at Everglades in Tommy's black Escalade at ten-fifty on Tuesday night. The buses were to pull up at eleven. They hoped to have all of the buses loaded and on their way to St. Stephens before eleven-thirty.

Grady Bardo's family day was just what the hard-working detective needed to recharge himself. He, his wife and son and daughter had attended mass that morning. His wife would be taking the kids out for back-to-school shopping.

Grady had picked up a couple of prime porterhouse steaks at his favorite butcher shop to grill that afternoon.

Once he had the house to himself, he changed into his trunks and settled into his floating chair in his pool with one of his favorite beers, a Hop Gun IPA from the Funky Buddha Brewery in nearby Oakland Park.

It was serene times like this that Bardo thought about how much he loved living and raising his family in South Florida: the near-daily blue skies with fluffy white clouds, the year-round lush greenery. Sure, it rained hard almost every afternoon this time of year, but the rains typically lasted for just a few minutes to a half-hour … then the sun was back.

His mind soon came back to his current primary case: the attempted murders of the Herreras and Jason Taylor. He was sure that he could eventually link Rebecca Cross to the shootings, but he first had to establish her motive: protecting her human trafficking activities.

The feds, not local authorities, were responsible for investigating and charging human trafficking cases, but he didn't want to take his suspicions to them yet. He didn't have enough evidence on Cross and he didn't want to complicate his own investigation at this point. Once he had evidence that Cross was involved in trafficking he would contact the FBI.

He decided he would start surveilling Cross more closely this week.

CHAPTER 34

John Herrera's doctor had told Di he could go home on Sunday. Di planned to go to the hospital after she and Jason had breakfast and sit with her mom and dad until John was discharged. She would then drive her dad home and stay with him as long as he needed her. John was instructed to stay off his wounded leg as much as possible for the first four or five days. The dressing on his wound needed to be changed daily during this time, as well.

Di wanted to use the time staying with her dad to rewrite and polish her story. An old college friend of Jason's, Bert Friedman, was now the Investigations Editor at the Miami Herald. Jason had pitched him Di's story, using the header, *Human trafficking and abuse uncovered at Broward child detention camp.* Bert had gotten back to him saying they were definitely interested in it. Jason told him that he thought her research would be complete by Wednesday and she hoped to have the story ready for submission by Wednesday afternoon.

Di planned to ask Jim Jeffries about the implications of including Jason's van photo with her story. Could the FBI or DHS search her devices and find the source of the photo? She would withhold the photo if it would mean the authorities would learn of Jason's and her involvement in the first rescue.

Staying at home with her dad for a while would also give Di time to reflect on what was happening between she and Jason. At this point could what they have even be called a relationship? They had really only been together for a little more than three days.

At this point, driving to the hospital, she couldn't help but think about Steve Martin in one of her favorite movies, *The Jerk*, saying to his new girlfriend, Marie, about their new relationship: "The first day seemed like a week. And the second day seemed like five days. And the third day seemed like a week again." She laughed and decided that, all things considered, she was pretty happy. She would call Jason once she got back home.

The more he thought about it, the more Jason realized he needed to tell Andru Mixon the real reason that he and his friends needed to be made up. He had to call him anyway to let him know that Tuesday would be the night. If things went south and they did get charged, Andru could potentially be an accomplice.

"Andru, this is Jason getting back to you about our make-up night."

"Happy Sunday to you, Jason. I'm just about to meet some friends for a bottomless mimosa brunch. We'd love if you could join us."

"Thanks a lot, Andru, but it's been a crazy few days. I'm

just going to be couching it today. Do you have a couple of minutes?"

"Of course."

"It looks like this Tuesday will be the night we'll need you. Probably around seven or eight. We'll need to be ready to leave here by ten."

"That works. I should get there by seven to have enough time for four of you."

"That's great, Andru. Say, I wasn't completely honest with you about our need to be disguised. We're not going to a costume party."

"No?"

"You can never repeat to anyone what I am about to tell you."

"Oh, a secret ... sounds exciting."

"This is serious, Andru. You can never tell *anyone*."

"You have my solemn word that I will not tell anyone."

"Okay, thanks. There is a detention facility for immigrant children about twenty miles west of here. We've learned that kids there are being sold to human traffickers, ten at a time."

"Oh my god!"

"And, they're being abused and drugged, and two of them have killed themselves."

"Jason! Have you reported them?"

"No. Reporting it wouldn't result in the kids being moved to anywhere safer. The four of us that you'll be disguising need to be unrecognizable as ourselves, even on video tape. We plan to bluff our way in posing as their bosses, Homeland

Security, doing a surprise inspection. We're then going to tell the administrator that all of the children are being transferred elsewhere. We have buses that will show up to pick up all of the children, and volunteers to shelter them in safe houses and church sanctuaries until we can reunite them with family members. We're consulting with the ACLU and they have said they'll represent us if anyone ends up getting charged."

"Jesus Christ, Jason."

"That's why I needed to tell you the truth. If we get identified and charged, the feds will probably want to know if anyone assisted with disguising us."

"What do you think those chances are?"

"Well, we wouldn't be doing it if we thought we were going to get caught. That's why you disguising us is so important."

"Count me in, Jason. If you and your friends are willing to put yourselves on the line for those kids, I am, too."

"That's great, Andru. We're in your debt. We'll see you at seven on Tuesday?"

"I'll be there. I looked up your address in the faculty directory. If this works, can I be made a junior Army Ranger?"

"Absolutely, Andru. I'll even get you a tan beret. Just remember, *no one* can know about this."

"I've got it, *no one*. I'll see you Tuesday at seven."

As soon as she got her dad home and settled, Di immediately took a long shower and changed into clean clothes. She felt reborn. Now she had to figure out the best way to clean the blood from the concrete garage floor and driveway. She thought of calling Jason, but she didn't want to be running to him for everything. So, she Googled, *how to clean blood off concrete*. The directions on the first site called for using something called sodium peroxide powder. It looked like she could only get this stuff from a chemical supply house and you'd just about need to wear a hazmat suit to work with it. Fortunately, the directions on the second site just called for rubber gloves, towels, a stiff-bristle scrubbing brush, liquid dish soap and hydrogen peroxide.

She decided she would have to change again, into something she wouldn't mind getting dirty. She moved all their cars out onto the street, careful to avoid the pool of Victor's dried blood on the driveway. She had avoided even looking at the dried pools of blood until now. As she knelt down next to where she had tended to her mother, she told herself it was just animal blood. That kind of worked, but she still had to concentrate to keep from gagging. She told herself that this was good experience, in a way: if she ever wrote a story that included the cleaning up of blood, she would have first-hand knowledge.

Neither of these avoidance techniques was really working. She found herself thinking instead of how much she loved her mother. How her mother, and father, had suffered terribly, and would continue to suffer, because of her. A few of her tears fell and mixed with the stains on the floor.

Di knew that neither of her parents blamed her. Just the same, she had to figure out some way to make up to them for this. The best way, she thought, would be for her to become a success. She wanted to make them proud of her, accomplish some things, move out on her own, be able to take care of them when they're older.

The first stain was as good as she could get it, at least for now. She used the hose and a power nozzle to spray the remnants out of the garage. She moved over to her father's large blood stain and started the process again. Suddenly, the heat in the garage was getting to her. She went inside to cool off, collect herself and drink some water.

Back in the garage, scrubbing at her father's blood, Di thought of his family: his refugee parents from Cuba were probably not all that different from the parents of the children held at Everglades. She realized she had to tell her father the whole story: the conditions at Everglades, the nighttime rescue, the plans for Tuesday night … everything.

An hour later she was finished with all three stains. She had actually caught herself smiling while cleaning up Victor's blood. She was happy that this lowlife sociopath wouldn't be stealing anymore children or shooting anymore innocent people. And Jason did it, she marveled. She had been so angry and frightened at the hospital that she told him he had to kill the shooters and he went right to her house and did it … killed one of them anyway. Jason was right, we do have a bond forged in fire, and now forged in blood.

She had to admit it, in only three days she had fallen hard for this man.

∽

Jason was thinking, too, as he sat at his kitchen table breaking down and cleaning his Beretta M9. He was listening to the original Twin Peaks soundtrack on a loop on his iPad. Jason and his friends had been addicted to Twin Peaks in junior high. He was especially taken with the character, Special Agent Dale Cooper. He remembered thinking back then how cool it would be to be an FBI special agent, investigating mysterious cases like the murder of Laura Palmer.

Well, here he was … in two nights he would get his chance to be an agent, of sorts. The dreamy music had him imagining he was slow dancing with Di at the Roadhouse, the infamous tavern that featured prominently in the series.

What *about* Di? Aside from all the violence and intrigue, they had been having a great time together. Jason had had girlfriends over the years, but it had always seemed like they were more into him than he was into them. They were the kind of relationships where he found himself saying, when they ended, "Its not you, its me." He hated feeling like he was letting a woman down. "You just haven't found the right one, yet," his mother would tell him at family gatherings. Was Di the right one? What would happen with them when this was all over? They hadn't even been on a real date yet. *"Be here now,"* he reminded himself.

He couldn't stop his mind, though. Maybe they would end up sitting together in a courtroom at a defendant's table. He knew he would protect Di at all costs. He could hear himself saying a variation of his old line, "it wasn't her, it was me."

Part of their plan was, if something went wrong, Father Pat and Catholic Charities would say that they were taking part in what they were led to believe was an authorized transfer of children. And Di would be on the first bus with Father Pat, so if that reasoning worked for the Church, it should work for her, a volunteer.

Jason recognized that he was thinking too much. He decided that once he was finished with his M9 he would turn on Netflix and find a good, escapist movie to watch. It dawned on him that he had gone pretty much the whole weekend without thinking about his classes or student papers. Would he have to tell Florida IT, "its not you, its me."? Maybe he and Di should become freelance investigative journalist partners. Maybe he should take Tommy Ziker up on his offer to become one of his "agents". Maybe he'd be sitting in a jail cell before the week was out.

CHAPTER 35

A fter four days Antonio was let out of isolation. Another bus load of children had arrived during his stay in the hot, windowless room. The cage was more crowded now. He wondered if there would even be a mat for him that night. He sensed that something else had changed in their cage community during his absence. Taunts were exchanged, arguments erupted, the boys seemed to have divided up based on country of origin.

Antonio knew that if the situation deteriorated further it would be bad for him, as well as for the rest of the caged boys. He stepped up onto one of the benches, waited for the talking to die down, and addressed the group: "Most of you here know me, you newcomers do not. My name is Antonio Vasquez. I am from San Pedro Sula, Honduras. I just got done spending five days in isolation for breaking up an assault on one of the young ones. While I was in isolation I did a lot of thinking. We, all of us, are in this together. We all made the long journey to the United States to escape the violence and fear in our home countries and to find a better life. Instead, we find ourselves in this cage, treated no better than animals. But we cannot allow ourselves to act like animals. We must stick together, look out for each other and care for each

SEPARATED AT THE BORDER

other. We won't be in here forever. There are Americans on the outside who are working to help us. I know this is so. We must have faith and not despair. I am not up here because I want to be your leader. I want all of us to be leaders. If you know some English you can help teach those of us who want to learn. If you have schooling you can help teach subjects to the younger ones. If you have lived in the United States before, you can teach those of us who haven't what life is like here. We cannot have any gang talk here. We have left the gangs behind. What I'm saying is that the best way for us to get through this temporary situation we find ourselves in is to respect each other and help each other. That is the best way for us to help ourselves."

Antonio paused and looked out at the faces watching him. "I hope I am not alone in believing this," he went on. "Raise your hand if you agree that we should all get along and help each other."

A few hands went up ... then a few more, soon all the boys were raising their hand.

"That's excellent," said Antonio. "I think a good start would be if all of us older boys would introduce ourselves to the younger boys. They are the most afraid and need our help the most. I will start."

Antonio stepped down and made a point to introduce himself to the youngest boy closest to him. They exchanged a few words and he then went on to the next child and did the same. Other older boys were following his lead.

The three guards in the control room were watching Antonio speak on their monitor but they had no idea what he was saying. "Looks like we have an agitator," said one.

"It's the one we just let out of isolation," said another.

"Maybe we should put the little prick back in," said the third.

"Let's hold off," said the second guard. "Who knows, maybe what he's saying will make our jobs easier."

"Whatever," said the first guard, and they went back to their card game.

CHAPTER 36

B y Monday Rebecca Cross was anxious to get back to work. She knew that Lt. Bardo had no jurisdiction at Everglades, so she would feel a lot safer there than she did sitting at home. She couldn't shake the feeling that he was watching her. In fact, Grady Bardo *was* parked on her street a few doors down, where she could not see his vehicle through any of her windows.

He had just taken a call from Frank Morrison telling him that the arraignments for Rico, Benny and Enrique were scheduled for later that morning and he would let him know their status once he found out the judge's ruling. He reminded Morrison to tell the Miami-Dade prosecutor that the three were also suspected in three attempted murders in Broward County last week and that their original intended target still fears for her life. Bardo didn't want them back on the street and hoped that this additional information would convince their judge to deny bail.

His next call was from the photo tech at his office telling him that she had made up new photo lineups that included Rico, Benny and Enrique's mugshots for showing to the Herreras.

He decided that Cross would probably not be going anywhere until she left for work sometime after three, so he headed for his office to pick up the photo lineups. In leaving, he made a point to drive slowly past Cross's townhouse, turn around and drive slowly past again on his way out of her community. He guessed, correctly, that she was watching out her front window.

He wasn't sure what time Robin Herrera's follow-up surgery was scheduled for today, so, after picking up the lineups he drove to the Herrera home to show one to John. The door was answered by Robin's sister, Heather Knox, who was just leaving for the hospital to sit with Robin. Bardo introduced himself and found out that Robin was already operated on earlier and was now in recovery. Di then came to the door, showed Bardo in and took him to her parents' bedroom.

"Dad, Lt. Bardo is here with another set of mugshots for you to look at," she told him.

"I'm sorry to barge in on you here at home, Mr. Herrera," said Bardo. "I brought another photo lineup for you to look at to see if you recognize the third shooter."

"No problem at all, lieutenant. It's good to have some male company," he said, winking at Di. "Let's have a look at your bad guys."

John took a long look and finally said, "sorry, lieutenant, none of these guys jumps out at me ... no pun intended. Like we said, they were pretty covered up and it was only a second or two before the bullets started flying."

"Well, its good to see you in this good a mood ... considering," said Bardo.

"I'll tell you something, lieutenant, you survive an attempt like that on your life, you *do* feel good. It would be a different story if Robin hadn't made it through, but after her surgery today, she should be well on the road to recovery, as well. Then again, it might just be the pain medication."

"I'm going to be weaning you off that pretty soon, dad," said Di. "You don't want to replace one problem with another."

"My daughter has become my mother," said John. "Lieutenant, thank you for coming by. I'm sorry I wasn't any help."

"Its good to see you're healing up, Mr. Herrera," said Bardo. "Thanks for looking at the photos. I'll be in touch."

Di walked Lt. Bardo to the front door. "So, do you still think Rebecca Cross was involved?" she asked.

"Absolutely," answered Bardo. "How else could the Dominican Kings have known who you are and where you live? Her cell phone shows calls going to and coming from both Victor Valbuena's phone, and his girlfriend Maria's phone."

"Will you be arresting her?" asked Di.

"Eventually, I'm sure. With Victor gone, *and* his little sidekick, it makes it harder for us to prove that Cross provided them with your address. I think Maria is our next best hope, but so far, she isn't talking. I'm going to keep working on her, though. I'll keep you informed."

Di thanked him, wished him luck and went back to her writing. She found it hard to concentrate, though. She kept thinking about Jason. She missed him. She missed waking up next to him. He would be at school now. Should she text him that she missed him? That's all he needs at work, she thought, some mushy text from me that makes him feel pressured to text me back. She decided instead to go with, *"Thinking about you. Hope you're having a good day. Call me after work."*

CHAPTER 37

There were emails from both the executive director *and* the president of the ACLU's national operations in New York waiting for Jim Jeffries when he arrived at his Miami office on Monday morning. Jeffries was executive director of the ACLU's Florida affiliate, but he needed the backing of officers and board members at the national level in order to secure approval to defend the rescuers of the detained Everglades children if it became necessary.

As he read them, he was not surprised that the leadership would not commit to assisting in a hypothetical future situation. Any ACLU assistance would hinge on, among other things, 1) whether trafficking and abuse at Everglades could be proven, 2) that no force was used in the removal of the children, and 3) that the identities and new locations of the children were fully documented. In addition, they indicated that Catholic Charities' decision to be involved reflected favorably on the operation.

To Jeffries, their response amounted to a big maybe. Personally, he still felt confident and committed. His new worry was that someone who now had access to the details of this plan would leak it to the government, or to the press, before Tuesday night.

That federal officials could be found to be complicit in the human trafficking of immigrant children taken by force from their families would reverberate through the government to the highest levels. This, he thought, could potentially be as big a scandal as Iran-Contra, the Pentagon Papers or Watergate.

Over the weekend, Jeffries had discussed this potential case with his wife, Abby, who works as the Chief Investment Officer for The Haskins Group, a large Miami-based money management firm. Abby had thought it best not to mention to Jim that some of her firm's important institutional clients were major stockholders in Detention Corporation of America. After wrestling with this conflict for most of Monday morning, Abby decided it was her fiduciary duty to advise these clients that the time might be right to sell off some of their DCA stock.

The resulting sell orders originating from Abby's firm triggered automated sell orders of DCA by other institutional investors. By the end of trading on Monday DCA stock was down more than twelve percent.

DCA management was shocked by the sell-off. The financial press was at a loss to explain the price drop. Rumors began to circulate that there may be some kind of serious problem with one of DCA's facilities.

DCA's chief financial officer, Tyler McReedy, traced the origin of the sell-off to Abby's firm in Miami. Once McReedy reported his findings to the rest of DCA management they began to suspect that the problem, whatever it was, had originated at one of their three facilities in South Florida. McReedy was tasked with beginning their investigation by phoning the chief administrators of those facilities late Monday afternoon.

∽

As usual, Rebecca Cross arrived at the Everglades Detention Center at four pm, went straight to her office and closed the door. She had a weekend's worth of paperwork to attend to but she couldn't bring herself to get started on it. All she could think about was the prospect of her new life in Micronesia. Maybe once she got there she could finally relax. It occurred to her that she couldn't remember the last time she felt really relaxed. She hadn't allowed herself to think in these terms before, but she could now admit to herself that she hated her job.

The last happiness she could remember was when she was promoted and transferred to Everglades. But that only lasted until she arrived at the place and experienced the sense of depression that hung over it like the stifling, humid South Florida air. You could smell the decay from the swamp as soon as you stepped outside.

She was jarred out of her reverie by the too-loud ringing of her desk phone.

"Everglades Detention Center, Chief Cross," she answered.

It was Tyler McReedy. "Chief Cross, hello, this is Tyler McReedy from DCA corporate. How is everything down there in South Florida?"

"Hello, sir. Everything here is running as smooth as a new pacemaker. How are you, sir?"

"I've been better, Chief Cross. Have you heard about where our stock closed today?"

"No sir, I haven't. A new high, I hope."

"Not exactly, chief. Our stock was down more than twelve percent today."

Cross could sense a storm cloud gathering. "Sounds like a good time to buy, then."

"Actually, I didn't call to discuss investment strategy, chief. Today's selloff of DCA stock began with a firm in Miami. No one seems to be able to put their finger on what triggered it, but since the selling began in Miami we're checking in with our facilities down there to see if you folks have any idea where any negative news may have originated."

"Like I said, sir, everything is running smoothly here. If there were a problem I would know about it."

"Be that as it may," said McReedy, "we'll be sending a team down to take a look at your facility, as well as our other two in South Florida."

"You know you folks are always welcome. When should we expect your team?"

"We don't know that yet for certain, chief. The best I can tell you is that you'll know when we pull up in front."

"Very good, sir. We look forward to greeting your team and showing them around."

Great, thought Rebecca after they hung up. As if I give a crap about their stock price. Hopefully I'll be long gone by the time they get here.

CHAPTER 38

By early Monday afternoon Jason was teaching his final class of the day. Ironically, this day's lesson was on the topic of journalistic ethics, regarding whether a reporter should become involved in the story he or she is covering. He told his students that The Society of Professional Journalists holds that, "journalists should report the story and not become a part of the story". "But," he continued, "being a journalist should not mean that you are no longer a human being with a conscience."

He shared with his students the standard examples of real-life exceptions to this rule: when Ed Bradley waded into the sea to help struggling refugees while covering a story; Sanjay Gupta providing medical assistance while covering stories of disease in third world countries; reporters giving a banana or a few pennies to starving children in Africa while covering famines.

He didn't include his former student's impending plan to rescue more than one hundred seriously at-risk children from a nearby government detention camp while writing a story about it. If his involvement ever became public he would have to alter this lesson next semester.

As class ended and he dismissed his students, Jason couldn't shake the gnawing feeling that something in his life was coming to an end. Or, maybe something was just beginning. Still at his desk, he took out his phone and called Di.

"Hey, mister," she answered. "I have some news for you."

"Hey, yourself. Tell me."

"The news is that I miss you. I miss you a lot."

"Then I guess you had better come over and let me make you dinner and spend the night."

Neither one said what they were trying not to think … that this might be the last night they would spend together for a long time if things didn't go as planned tomorrow.

"That's exactly what I was hoping you would say. I'm going to make some dinner for my dad, get changed and I'll be on my way."

"I'm going to stop at the store on the way home. Any requests?"

"Surprise me. See you in an hour or so?"

"See you then," said Jason. "I miss you, too."

By Monday afternoon, Lt. Bardo had been to All Souls again and shown the new lineup to Robin Herrera. She, too, was unable to recognize any of them.

Back in his car, he noticed that it was now after four and Rebecca Cross would be back in her office. He called her cell number, rather than her office phone. She could see it was he calling her. She had only been off her office phone for a few minutes, following her conversation with Tyler McReedy.

"Yes, lieutenant?" she answered, not caring if she sounded exasperated.

"Chief Cross, I'm following up on my request to you for the home address and phone number for Tony Lopez."

"Hold on." She brought up Captain Tony's information on her computer and read it off to Bardo. "Is that it, then?" she asked him when finished.

"Just about. What are Captain Lopez's hours at Everglades?"

Cross picked a hard candy out of the bowl on her desk. She wanted to crunch it right in his ear. "He works the same shift as I do, four to midnight, Monday through Friday." She popped the candy into her mouth and crunched hard.

"Thank you, Chief. I'll be in touch," finished Bardo, before jerking his phone away from his ear. He made a mental note to call her on speaker next time.

The first thing Cross had to do, after her back-to-back phone calls, was to get Captain Lopez into her office and bring him up to speed on the suspicious Lt. Bardo and the phony job-seeking story she had told him. She texted him to come to her office, rather than using the facility-wide intercom. She didn't like hearing the sound of her voice echoing off the walls.

"Captain Lopez," she began, after he had arrived in her office. Even though they were partners in crime, Cross never dropped the formality. It was never, 'Tony'. "There's nothing to worry about," she continued, "but a Broward County police detective has been asking me questions." She saw Lopez stiffen. "Please, sit down, Captain," she said, motioning to the standard-issue gray government chair across the desk from where she was seated. "I don't know if you saw the news over the weekend, but the individual who has been picking up our shipments was shot and killed in Dania Beach."

"No shit? Victor was killed?"

Cross scribbled furiously on a piece of paper and held it up to him. "NO NAMES!!!", it read. "This detective ... Bardo," she went on, "also told me that this individual shot and almost killed two people at the same address a couple of hours earlier." Cross was now slowly folding the piece of paper over and over, staring at it. "The detective told me that my office and cell phone numbers were found on this individual's phone." She stopped folding and looked back up at Tony. "Of course, I explained to him how this individual had approached you at the gym, saying he was trying to help his cousin get a job." Tony's eyes were starting to widen. "And I explained that you had wanted to help and had given this individual my office number so he could call and inquire about a job. And you ..."

"You told him what?" Tony whisper-screamed.

"Anyway, I just got off the phone with this Lt. Bardo," Rebecca went on. "He wanted your address and phone number so you could confirm my story."

"This is not good, Chief."

"Listen, its not a problem as long as we tell him the same story."

"Not a problem? How about when this cop talks to Victor's cousin ..."

Cross held her finger to her lips.

"Screw no names," hissed Lopez. "He obviously knows Victor's name since he's been asking you about him. So, you've talked to Victor's cousin and told him this story he's supposed to tell?"

"No," said Cross. "I want you to talk to him. I'm not going back over to that neighborhood."

Lopez started to speak, but Cross cut him off, "I'm even going to give you the rest of the day off so you can go over there now."

"Go where?" asked Lopez. "I don't know where any of them live."

"Lucky for you I have their address in my phone," said Rebecca, taking out her phone and bringing up the address Victor had given her three nights before. She slid the phone and a piece of paper and pen across her desk. "There you go, write it down."

Lopez gave her a hard look, wrote down the address and then stood up. "Is that all?"

Rebecca stood, as well. "That address is a fourplex," she said. "The cousin lives in the unit second from the left."

"How do you know that?"

"The night I dropped them off I waited and watched which doors they each went into."

Lopez considered asking her why she would do that, but he didn't want to prolong his time in her office. Instead, he put the address in his pocket and turned to go.

As he did, Cross said to him, "I think his name is Manuel."

"No, it's Miguel," said Lopez, on his way out of her office.

Captain Lopez retrieved his uneaten bag lunch from his cubicle in the control room and headed to the parking lot. He had just started his car and adjusted the A/C when his phone rang. He didn't recognize the local number on its display and figured it was another damn robocall.

"Hello."

"Is this Anthony Lopez?" asked the male voice on the other end.

"Who is this?" asked Tony.

"I'm Detective Lieutenant Grady Bardo with the Broward County Sheriff's department. I have a few questions for you."

"This isn't a good time, I'm driving in heavy traffic," lied Tony.

"Let's meet somewhere then. Where are you?"

"I'm going east on I-75 in Weston."

"Okay, there's a Denny's at the Weston Road exit. Meet me there in fifteen minutes."

"Is this really necessary, Lieutenant?" asked Lopez.

"Well, Captain, you are a person of interest in three at-tempted murders in Dania Beach last week so, yeah, it *is* necessary ... unless you would rather be questioned at headquarters."

"First of all, I have no idea what you're talking about but, okay, I'll meet you at Denny's. I'm wearing my uniform."

Bardo was already seated at a booth facing the door when he saw Tony Lopez walk in. He raised his arm and motioned him over. Bardo stood, introduced himself, discretely showed Tony his badge and they sat down.

"What's this b.s. about three attempted murders?" Tony asked.

"I assure you, it's not b.s.," said Bardo. "First, though, I have to confirm some information that Rebecca Cross gave me over the weekend."

"That woman has quite an imagination," said Tony. "What did she tell you?"

"Why do you say she has quite an imagination?"

"I'll just say she's not the most truthful person I've ever known."

"I see. Do you two not get along?"

"I do my job, she does hers. We get along okay."

A waitress came to their booth and they both ordered coffee.

"Do you know Victor Valbuena?" Bardo asked after she left.

"We worked out at the same gym so, yeah, I knew him"

"You said that in the past tense. So, you know he was killed?"

"Yeah, I heard about it. No big loss, in my opinion."

"What about his cousin?"

"What *about* his cousin?" countered Tony.

"Chief Cross told me that you were trying to help Victor's cousin get a job at Everglades."

"Yeah, Victor mentioned that to me."

"And you gave him Cross's phone number?"

"I might have. I don't really remember. What does this have to do with three attempted murders?"

"Are you aware that a Diamond Herrera was a volunteer translator at Everglades last week?"

"I know someone came and translated. I didn't get her name."

"Well, two days after she translated at Everglades, Victor and two of his Dominican Kings buddies went to Ms. Herrera's home and shot and seriously wounded her parents, mistaking her mother for Ms. Herrera." Bardo made note of Tony's impassive reaction to hearing this. "Then, two hours later, Victor returned alone and attempted to kill Ms. Herrera's friend. Her friend was armed, returned fire, and killed Victor."

"Victor never was the brightest bulb in the chandelier," was Tony's response. "I still don't see how this involves me."

"The only connections between Ms. Herrera and Victor Valbuena are Rebecca Cross and you." Bardo could tell that Lopez was thinking.

"I sure as hell didn't tell Victor, or anyone else, to kill anybody."

"No? You didn't suspect that Ms. Herrera had learned about the human trafficking out of Everglades, and you didn't tell Victor to eliminate that threat?"

"What the hell?" said Tony. "You're out of your mind. I don't even know this Ms. Herrera."

"Then it was Rebecca Cross who put the hit out on her?"

Tony shook his head. "I can't believe that. Human trafficking … that's crazy."

"I tell you what," said Bardo, his voice lowered and leaning across the table. "You need to get yourself a good lawyer and start working with me to help solve this. That's the only way to minimize your jeopardy. You can bet your boss won't have your back when this all goes bad. My guess is that she'll try to pin this whole thing on you."

Bardo took one of his cards out and slid it across the table to Tony. "I thought you worked the four to midnight shift, Captain. Did Chief Cross send you on an errand? Maybe to go find Victor's cousin and get your stories straight?"

Tony couldn't tell how much this lieutenant knew or how much he was guessing.

"I wasn't feeling well," said Tony. "Cross told me to go home for the rest of the day."

"Well, I'm heading over to Little Santo Domingo right now to talk to Victor's cousin," said Bardo. "Is there any message you want me to give him?"

Tony coughed a couple of times. "Why the hell would I want you to give him a message? I only met him one time when he came to the gym with Victor."

Bardo stood. "Okay. Coffee's on me," as he dropped a five on the table. "I hope you start feeling better. Give me a call after you've thought about this a little more."

As he sat in the booth and watched Bardo walk out of Denny's, Tony Lopez realized he *was* feeling sick ... sick with fear.

CHAPTER 39

A s soon as Di stepped into Jason's condo she could smell something good. Jason came from the kitchen to greet her.

"You really *are* cooking for me," she said, as they embraced.

"I hope you're ready for my grouper extravaganza," he said, just before a prolonged kiss. After the kiss, they continued to hold each other, neither speaking.

When they finally parted, Di said, "It smells wonderful. Show me."

"I guess I should have asked you first if you like grouper," said Jason as they walked to the kitchen.

"Come on, Jason. What Florida girl doesn't like grouper?"

Grouper, a member of the sea bass family, is a Florida favorite, with eighty percent of U.S. production harvested off Florida's shores.

"And *wine*," said Di, noticing the bottle of white wine chilling in an ice bucket on Jason's kitchen island.

Jason lifted the dripping bottle from the ice and began pouring two glasses. "My wine guy told me this is the best accompaniment with grouper," he said. "It's a 2017 pinot gris from Oregon."

"I didn't know you had a wine guy," said Di. "Who is it?"

"Actually, it's the closest clerk to the wine section when I'm at Total Wine."

Jason poured them each a glass and they toasted. "Here's to tonight," said Jason.

"And tomorrow," toasted Di. She looked over at Jason's dining table, set with cloth napkins and a single red rose in a glass bud vase. "Jason, everything is beautiful. You're going to spoil me ... and this wine is perfect."

"What can I say ... you inspire me," said Jason, removing the shallow pan with the sizzling fillets from the oven. "Go sit down and I'll serve you."

He placed a fillet on each plate, then added steamed broccoli and mashed potatoes from saucepans on the stove. The final touch was his homemade tarter sauce in a small bowl that he retrieved from the refrigerator.

"Are you sure you're the same guy who wears camo, hides in the brush and takes down bad guys?" Di asked him before taking her first bite of grouper.

"Same guy," said Jason. "And you had better mind your manners tonight or I might just take you down."

"Promises, promises," said Di, laughing.

Jason took a sip of wine, staring at her. "Did you know you're beautiful when you eat?" he asked.

Di opened her mouth while chewing broccoli. "Still think so?"

Jason tossed a floret at her mouth. "I'm sorry," she said. "That wasn't a very nice way to take a compliment. I should have said, 'and you, sir, are very handsome at *all* times.' That's what I was thinking."

They went on to talk about how Di's parents were doing, Jason's day at school, etc. When they were done with dinner Di helped carry the dishes to the sink, Jason opened another bottle of wine and they settled in on the living room couch.

Di turned to face him, sitting sideways with her feet pulled up under her, holding her wine glass in one hand and pushing her long, black hair back over her right shoulder with the other. "Tell me more about yourself, Jason. Before you were a professor. Before you were a Ranger."

Jason told her about growing up in Doral, attending and playing football at Miami Springs High, playing tight end for the University of Miami Hurricanes football team on a scholarship.

"You played for the U?" Di exclaimed, suddenly sitting up straight. "Why didn't you tell me? The 'Canes are my favorite college team! A tight end ... you *look* like a tight end. Oh my god, did you play for the national championship team in '01?"

Jason was smiling at how Di was going on. "I played *on* it. But 2001 was the year 9/11 happened. Genius me, I left school, left football and enlisted."

"Are you glad you did? Or, do you regret it?"

"Both. I figured we had a good chance to win the Big East, like we did the year before. To be honest, it never crossed my mind that the team might win it all that year when I made the decision to enlist."

"I remember when I was about five," said Di, "I think it was in 1999 – my folks got me a 'Canes cheerleader outfit for Halloween. I didn't want to take it off. I think I even wore it to school one day." Di stopped abruptly. Jason sensed she was thinking. Finally, "So, when I was five, you were one year away from playing college ball. How old *are* you, Jason?"

"I'm thirty-five."

"That's good. I like my men experienced," said Di, looking over the top of her wine glass at him and doing her best Latina Mae West impression. She took a sip, "Seriously, I can't wait to tell my parents you played tight end for the U."

"I would have led with that if I had known you were a football groupie. Okay, your turn. Tell me all about Diamond."

"Well, I've lived all my life in the same house in Dania Beach. I went to South Broward High. I was a cheerleader my last two years … go Bulldogs! I've known since grade school that I wanted to be a journalist. Then, while I was in middle school, there was a reporter with the Herald, Debbie Cenziper, who won the Pulitzer for investigative reporting. She was kind of my role model for what I wanted to become." She took another sip of her wine. "It's taking too long, though. I thought I'd have a staff job somewhere by now."

"Do you want some advice?" asked Jason.

"Yes. Please."

"I think you should specialize in a topic that the cable news shows talk about. Once you've established some expertise on a subject, you would be a natural to be an on-air talking head. While you were talking just now, I couldn't take my eyes off you."

"Really?"

"Even if you don't see it yet, I can. You definitely have what it takes. I snuck a few peeks at what you've been writing. It's really good. It's clear that you're passionate, yet truthful. You've improved a lot since you were in my class."

"I can feel my head swelling. Go on."

"Take what we're involved with right now: immigration, family separations, detentions, reunifications, human trafficking, gang activity. Those are huge news topics, both locally and nationally. If your story about all of this gets picked up by the Herald on Wednesday, I wouldn't be surprised if TV news operations will want to interview you about it. Hell, you might even need to get an agent."

"If I do need one, *you* could be my agent, Jason. We *are* a team, right?"

"We *are* a team," said Jason, taking her hand.

"That reminds me," said Di. "I've been meaning to ask you if you'll be my editor on the story."

"I would be honored to be your editor."

"Alright! So, you're going to be my agent *and* my editor. And, since you're a tight end, I feel like I'm in *very* good hands." She stood and pulled Jason to his feet. "Is it ethical for a girl to sleep with her agent *and* her editor at the same time?"

"I'm pretty sure it is," said Jason. "As long as you don't write about it."

CHAPTER 40

The first thing Tony Lopez did after Bardo left was to call Rebecca Cross to tell her that the lieutenant had intercepted him on his way to Little Santo Domingo, and that Bardo was now on his way there to find and question Miguel.

The only thing that Cross said was, "Shit!", before hanging up. She wondered if Bardo really did have her office bugged. To be safe, she walked outside before calling Maria from her Burner number. By now, Maria recognized that the incoming blocked number was Cross.

"What is it?" answered Maria. She had her hands full at the moment feeding pureed rice and beans to Eddie in his high chair.

"You know who this is?" asked Cross.

"Yes, I know who this is. I'm busy. What do you want?"

"I want you to listen carefully," said Cross. "That lieutenant from Broward County is on his way over there to question Victor's cousin." Even though it was a little after five p.m., it was still ninety-five degrees out … *and* humid as hell. Standing in the parking lot, Cross was already sweating through her brown uniform shirt and breathing through her mouth, trying to avoid the fetid swamp smell.

"Why should I care?" said Maria, trying to get the baby to take another spoonful.

"Listen," said Cross, "You need to find Victor's cousin and tell him to tell the cop that Victor and he called me to ask about a job at Everglades."

"Victor wanted a job at Everglades? Who's going to believe that?"

"No, not Victor ... his cousin wanted a job here. That's the story I gave the lieutenant. Victor's cousin has to tell him the same story or we're all in trouble."

"I'm not in trouble. I haven't done anything. And Victor can't get in any more trouble. So, what you're really saying is that you want me to do this for you. I think *you* need to come over here and talk to Miguel yourself."

"There's no time. The cop is on his way there now. Can you just go find Miguel and let me talk to him on your phone?"

"I told you, I'm busy."

"Do you know a number I can call, then, to talk to Miguel?"

Maria was better at assessing situations than Victor had been. She knew there was no upside to giving Carlotta's number to Cross. "No, I don't have a number. But we still have a deal for tomorrow night. I'm going to be there at eleven, like we arranged."

Cross didn't want to risk angering the gang by not going through with the Tuesday night pickup. Plus, she needed the cash she would receive for the children. "Yes, it's still on, but you need to do your part to make sure it can happen. I know that Miguel just lives next door. After we hang up, please go over there and tell him what he needs to say."

"Yeah, okay. If he's home I'll tell him."

"That Victor and he called my office number and cell number because Miguel wanted a job at Everglades. Thank you, Maria."

Maria cleaned Eddie off, lifted him out of the chair and walked over to Carlotta's. Miguel was lying on the couch watching a soccer match on TV. After Carlotta let her in, Maria told Miguel about the call she just received and what Cross wanted him to say to Bardo.

"Yeah, whatever," was Miguel's response.

Once again, Lieutenant Bardo was calling Frank Morrison to see if he was available to accompany him on his visit to Allapattah ... this time to interview Miguel. Lt. Morrison told him he was close to wrapping up an interview not far from there and would meet him at Rico's at six.

Miguel was still on the couch watching soccer when the two detectives arrived. Carlotta answered the door and told Miguel to talk to them outside, claiming the detectives were bad luck and she didn't want them in her house.

"So, tell me about Rebecca Cross," Bardo asked him, once the young DK was outside.

Miguel answered without looking at either of them, "I wanted to get a job from her, working at her detention camp."

"Was Victor involved in that?" Bardo asked him.

"Yeah, Victor called her, and then I called her."

"Where did you call her?"

"I don't know, at her work I guess."

"So, did you get a job?" asked Bardo.

"I don't know yet."

"Do *you* have a phone?"

"Yeah, I got a phone," answered Miguel.

"Why didn't you call Cross on your phone? Or give her your number to call you back on?"

"Because it was Victor's idea. I didn't even want a job there."

"You just told me you called Cross because you wanted a job at her detention center."

"I was pretending … for Victor. He thought he was doing me a favor, so I went along with it, but I didn't really want to work there."

Bardo was wondering how Cross had gotten to Miguel so he would know how to answer his questions. He tried a different approach. "You know it's a serious federal crime to buy and sell children, right? Punishable by twenty-five years or more in prison." Miguel said nothing. "Victor's not around to protect anymore, and Rico's in jail on a murder charge. You have to look out for yourself now, Miguel. You don't have to tell me anything about the DK's, I'm only interested in Cross."

Miguel had folded his arms and was looking past them, saying nothing. He had overheard Carlotta talking to Maria earlier about doing another pickup. He wasn't going to snitch out his step-mother. He took the card that Bardo held out to him only because he hoped that the detective would leave if he did so.

"Miguel, I'm trying to help you. Take my card and call me after you've thought about this awhile," said Bardo, trying to make eye contact with him.

"You should listen to the lieutenant," said Morrison. "I don't know why, but he really is trying to help you."

"Is that all?" said Miguel.

"That's all for now," said Bardo. "We'll be talking to you again, one way or another."

CHAPTER 41

J ason and Di got up at the same time early Tuesday morning. Jason made his famous toast again ... this time topped with local orange marmalade. After eating, Di poured some coffee into one of Jason's Miami Hurricanes travel mugs, kissed him and left to tend to her dad. Neither talked about what would happen tonight. They both knew that all elements of the rescue were in place ... talking about it now might be a jinx. Jason packed his class work into his dark brown leather flapover briefcase and left for school a few minutes later.

It was a beautiful South Florida morning: deep blue skies and just a few white puffball clouds ... a sign of lower humidity. There was no such thing as *low* humidity in this part of the state in the late summer, but even slightly lower humidity was some relief.

Once she arrived home, Di would fix breakfast for her dad, change the dressing on his leg wound, do a load of wash, and keep him company for a while before heading to the hospital to visit her mother.

Di's aunt, Heather, was still staying with them and spending her days at the hospital with Robin. Di had gotten the distinct impression that Heather blamed her for the shooting of her parents. In fact, John had told Di that Heather had tried that line of accusatory thinking on him. He said that he had told her, in so many words, to shove it. Di already felt terrible about what had happened – she didn't need her nose-in-the-air Aunt Heather trying to turn her parents against her.

Di had picked up a bed table for her dad on Sunday so he wouldn't have to have anything lying on his lap and irritating his wound. Between bites of his bacon and eggs and toast, John told Di how he had discovered Google Earth on his laptop the day before and had been cruising down streets in cities around the world ever since. She waited until he finished describing the ultra-modern cities he had been to in China before beginning the full story of her and Jason's involvement with the Dominican Kings and the Everglades Detention Center.

John was shocked, but proud, of his daughter's involvement. When she got to the part about the rescue of the van full of children in the middle of the night, she brought up Jason's photo on her phone and showed him.

"My god, Diamond, no wonder they were after you," he said while looking at it.

"Jason's private detective friend put a GPS tracker under their van before they brought it back to the gang. It was programmed to give an alert on the phone of each of us involved if the van got within two miles of any of our homes. The alert went off on my phone. That's how I knew to call and warn you."

"Too bad he didn't set it to go off at four or five miles," said John as he finished off his last strip of bacon. "Why did they even bring the van back to them?"

"They showed the gang leader – he owned the van – the photo and warned that if there was any attempted retribution, they would go straight to the FBI with it."

"I guess that didn't work out so good," said John. "So, did they take the photo and information to the FBI?"

"No. Actually, we have a better plan for helping the children."

"What would that be?" asked John before taking a sip of his orange juice.

"We're going to rescue *all* the children from Everglades tonight."

John's reaction almost sprayed juice onto Di. "Honey, don't get involved in this any further. I know you mean well, but you're in way over your head. My god, look what's happened so far. It would kill your mother and I if you got hurt … or worse."

"Really, it's a genius plan, dad. There are so many good people who have volunteered to help. The gang is not involved … they're all dead or in jail. In fact, my only involvement will be riding in a charter bus with a Catholic priest."

"The church is involved now?"

"Yes, Catholic Charities, the ACLU, Jason and his detective friends. And I'm writing the story about it for the Miami Herald."

Di went on to tell her dad the details of the plan.

"So, you probably won't get shot," he said, "but it sounds like there's a decent chance you could get arrested."

"Even if it did come to that, the ACLU said they will probably represent us, and there's a good chance they would win the case."

"Probably? A good chance? Oh, my sweet girl … you know I've never been a religious man, but I'm going to start praying for you right now. Promise me you won't tell your mother any of this."

"I promise I won't … but I needed to tell you. I would have felt dishonest if I hadn't. I love you, dad," she said, bending down and kissing John on the forehead. "Try not to worry too much. I'll be back here at the same time tomorrow to take care of you."

"You know I won't be able to sleep tonight. Be sure you call me when it's over and you know you're safe. I don't care how late it is. I love you, too, sweetie."

Rebecca Cross spent Tuesday morning cleaning her town-house, doing laundry and packing for her move the next day to her new life in Micronesia. Late in the morning she took a break and drove to her bank. She withdrew her entire life savings of six thousand and forty-four dollars, less twenty dollars. She left the twenty dollars in her account, fearing that closing it might trigger some kind of an alert to the authorities.

When she got back home, she distributed the cash evenly into the four bags she was bringing, plus her purse. Having the cash meant that she wouldn't have to use her credit cards until she had been in Micronesia for awhile. Even with the three thousand she would receive tonight, she would still be under the ten-thousand-dollar limit that would require her to declare her cash to customs.

She knew she should have started this process sooner, but with all the nervous energy she was feeling, she was getting a lot done. She would tell the realtor she selected that they could take whatever they wanted from the house, except for the furniture. She would sell the townhouse furnished.

By three p.m. she was pretty well packed and ready to go. She took a shower, put on her brown DCA uniform and headed to work. She hoped to hell that this wouldn't be the day that Tyler McReedy's DCA team showed up for their inspection. One of her first orders of business would be to select the two boys and eight girls that she would sell to Maria tonight.

Storm clouds were gathering in the east as Rebecca parked her F-150 and walked into Everglades Detention Center for the last time at a little before four p.m. After she was buzzed through the front doors and got to her office, she retrieved the Spanish translation of, *"We have located your family member. You will be leaving tonight to reunite with them,"* that she had printed out the day of the first sale of children.

She then walked down the white corridor and told control to buzz her into the cage room. She walked to the boys' cage first and peered through the chain link mesh. Most of the fifty-two boys were lounging on their mats or sitting on the benches.

"Everyone stand up," she ordered. *"Todos se levantan,"* called out one of the boys who knew English and hoped that his spontaneous translations might earn him favor. The boys slowly rose to their feet.

∞

Antonio had only seen Rebecca Cross a few times since his arrival, but he knew that she ran the place. As he stood with the others, he wondered what special occasion caused her to visit them. As she slowly looked over the boys, Antonio could see that her eyes had settled on him. She pointed at him and motioned to him to come over to her. She did the same thing with Adalberto, and soon the two boys were at the fence looking up at her large, impassive face.

Cross looked down at her paper and read – in terrible Spanish, *"Hemos localizado a su familiar. Saldrás esta noche para reunirte con ellos."* ("We have located your family member. You will be leaving tonight to reunite with them")

The two boys broke out in large smiles and hugged each other. *"Muchas gracias",* "Thank you, thank you," they said to Cross. But she had already turned her back and was calling Captain Lopez, who was watching the selection play out from the control room.

"These two will be leaving tonight, Captain. Get their names, remove them from the system and have them ready to go by ten." She then walked to the girls' cage and went through the same process, picking out the eight most attractive girls who looked eleven or older.

CHAPTER 42

Tuesday morning found Grady Bardo at his desk tying up some loose ands and completing paperwork on a couple of his older cases the DA was preparing for trial. Foremost on his mind, though, was finding out the truth about Rebecca Cross. He needed to talk to Di Herrera's source for the trafficking information, Tomas Suarez. He called Di while she was on her way to All Souls. After pulling over, she looked up Reina's number on her phone and gave it to him.

After the arrests of Rico, Enrique and Benny, Reina and Tomas felt it was no longer necessary for Tomas to go into hiding at their sister's in Orlando. Instead, he was busy making multiple trips moving his belongings from his apartment to Reina's home. Tomas was at Reina's when Bardo's call came through. Tomas told the lieutenant he was willing to talk and Bardo told him he would be to Reina's at one o'clock.

When Bardo arrived, Reina asked him if he minded if she be present for the interview. Bardo told her that would be fine. She removed her clay- and paint-stained work apron and they sat down in the same living room where the rescue had been planned out three days earlier.

Bardo placed his digital recorder on the coffee table between them and pressed record. "Tomas, I want to thank you for agreeing to talk with me today about your time at Everglades," said Bardo. "I want you to know that, at this point, everything you say to me will be held in confidence. Unless and until this goes to trial, no one at Everglades, or with the Dominican Kings, will know that we talked."

"Okay," said Tomas.

"Diamond Herrera told me that when she interviewed you, you described human trafficking – the sale of children – taking place at Everglades. Is that the case?"

"There were rumors," said Tomas. "If it *is* true, Chief Cross is definitely involved. I'm guessing it's just her and Captain Lopez. The rumors started with the guards who work the night shift. The way it's supposed to work is, Cross picks out around ten kids, mostly girls, who are supposed to be leaving to be reunited with their family members they crossed the border with." Tomas was back to fiddling with his ear lobe expanders. "The thing is, the pickups supposedly happen at the back door, at around midnight, and only Chief Cross and Lopez are involved in turning them over."

"So, you did not witness any of these departures?" asked Bardo.

"No. By the time I heard anything, it was second- and third-hand rumors."

"Did any of these rumors include a description of the vehicle involved?"

"No. I heard that only Cross and Lopez went out the back door, and the other guards weren't even allowed in the back hallway at those times."

"How many pickups like this do you think happened while you were still working there?"

"Possibly one or two."

Bardo went on to ask Tomas about physical and sexual abuse at Everglades, as well as the administering of drugs and the two suicides. Tomas told him the same things he had related to Di on Thursday. Bardo made a note to check how far DCA's property line extended behind the facility. It might be possible that the two suicide victims are buried on public land, in which case Bardo could come back in the morning with a cadaver dog team to look for the graves.

"So, would it be accurate to say that you are in fear of Chief Cross?" Bardo asked him.

"Yeah, after what happened to Di's parents, I worry that someone could come after me because Cross suspects that I was responsible for Reina's demonstration and the news coverage. I don't think she would do anything herself, but she sure seems to be tied in with that gang."

"You mean the Dominican Kings?"

"If they're the ones that shot Di's parents, yeah."

"Well, two of those three are dead and we're fairly certain the third shooter is one of the DK's in the Miami-Dade jail with no bond, along with the one who was calling the shots."

"Still, I'll sleep better when I know that Cross is out of the picture."

"We're still gathering facts and we'll see where they take us," said Bardo. "I have one last question, and this is for both of you ... a couple of days ago, when I was questioning Rico

Valbuena, he said he thought I had been shown a photo that I have to believe has to do with this case. He then refused to answer any of my questions about this photo. Would either of you know what he was referring to?"

Reina and Tomas looked at each other briefly and Reina spoke first. "Nothing comes to mind, lieutenant."

"The only picture I can think of is the one Cross showed me on her laptop of Reina at the demonstration," answered Tomas.

Bardo turned off his recorder, stood and thanked them for their time. Back in his car, he was thinking about the glance Reina and Tomas had given each other before answering his question about the photo. He felt certain that these two, as well as Di Herrera and Jason Taylor, knew more than they were telling him. A lot of it probably had to do with that photo … but he guessed there was more, as well. Were they protecting themselves? Or somehow trying to protect the kids at Everglades? Although he didn't suspect them of any wrongdoing, he decided that, just to be thorough, he would run background checks on each of them when he got back to his office.

⚭

After sitting with her mother – and Heather – for a couple of hours at the hospital, Di drove to Jason's. Jason was still at school so she let herself in. She had brought more of her clothes with her and, after hanging them up in Jason's closet, she began thinking about how, with each passing day, she was coming closer and closer to moving in with him. They had formed a real bond over just four days. Was she falling in love with him, she wondered? Had she already fallen in love with him?

And, how deep were his feelings for her? She was imagining that tomorrow morning, after a successful rescue, he could tell her, "It was really great getting to know you better, Di. You'll have to stay in touch." After all, it was she that had put the first move on him. Maybe he had just been being polite ... not wanting to hurt the feelings of an infatuated former student.

"Stop it," she told herself. This was not the day to get all twisted up trying to figure out a four-day relationship. "Be here now, Di." She knew she needed to occupy her mind, so she opened her laptop on the breakfast bar and started editing her yet-to-be-finished story.

Jason arrived home thirty minutes later. Her worries disappeared when he immediately walked over to her with a big smile saying, "Di, I was hoping you'd be here," and wrapped her in a long, tight hug. The kiss that followed had her feeling silly for doubting his feelings for her ... and hers for him.

"I would crack open a couple of beers or a bottle of wine, but we've got a long night ahead of us," he said. "So how about a bottle of water?"

"That sounds perfect. What time are Tommy and his guys getting here?"

"They, and Andru, are supposed to get here at seven."

"I'm anxious to see if I'll be able to recognize you after he's done," she said. "It'll be like Halloween, but without the candy."

CHAPTER 43

———～～———

By a little after seven, Tommy, Hector, Joe and Andru were at Jason's and ready to get started with their preparations. Andru positioned Jason's four dining area chairs side-by-side and adjusted the lighting so that there would be maximum light on their faces. He had brought his large, four-tier professional makeup case on wheels which he positioned next to the four men. Di had turned Jason's easy chair around so she could sit and watch Andru work. Jason started playing a Bob Marley mix on his iPad and they were ready to go.

Andru meticulously arranged his materials on Jasons dining table: rubbing alchohol, cotton balls, Q-tips, powder, spirit gum and medical adhesive, nose putty, liquid latex, castor oil sealer, cream base color, highlight, shadows, colored contact lenses, final seal, and adhesive remover. The three large lower drawers in his case were filled with his extensive selection of latex facial prosthetics. All four men were seated with makeup bibs in place.

"Hey Andru, can you make me look like DeNiro?" asked Joe.

"I'll go for the Antonio Banderas look," added Hector, "My wife would love it."

"I wish I would have had time to make face molds of you guys so I could have pre-fitted a lot of these prosthetics," said Andru. "But, fortunately for you, I am a consummate professional and can overcome this minor issue." He took a close look at Jason's face. "Jason, would you mind terribly shaving off that stubble? I can do a lot more with you if your skin is smooth. Hector and Joe, you can keep your beards … unless you *want* to shave." Neither did.

Andru started with Tommy. He first wiped Tommy's face with rubbing alcohol to remove skin oil..He next took out a wrap-around face prosthetic that featured a larger nose and fuller cheeks. Andru had decided to use medical adhesive to secure the latex prosthetics to their faces, rather than spirit gum which can loosen and slip in warm, humid conditions. He first did a test fitting to make sure it was the right size for Tommy's face. It fit.

Jason returned to the group freshly shaven. Di jumped up to feel his face before Andru started working on him. "Hey, I think I like this," she said, holding his face in her hands and giving him a kiss. She remained with the group of men so she could more closely watch Andru at work.

Andru next began applying the medical adhesive under the edges and on Tommy's skin, starting in the middle of his face, above and at the bottom of his nose. He waved his hands to dry it a little, then pressed it down. He repeated these steps, moving outward toward the edges until the prosthetic was firmly in place. He then blended the edges to his face with liquid latex and applied just enough base makeup to make it look real. As a final touch, Andru applied prosthetic bushy black eyebrows and a fake goatee that was flecked with gray. They all agreed that Andru knew what he was doing … Tommy was unrecognizable, but natural looking.

Jason went next. His face would take longer than Hector or Joe's, since they had full beards. Andru selected a prosthetic chin, some dental plumpers to slightly expand his cheeks, blue contacts to put over his brown eyes, and what all agreed looked like a porn star mustache. He set it off with a pair of wire-rim glasses with no correction.

It was a little after eight-thirty, and Andru already was done with his two most time-consuming subjects. Di was about to take Jason's picture when the doorbell rang.

"Are you expecting anyone?" Tommy asked.

"No," said Jason. "Di, would you mind getting that? Tell them we don't need any."

Di went to the door and opened it. "Lieutentant Bardo," she exclaimed, loud enough for all to hear. "What can I do for you?" she asked, standing in the open doorway. She could see that Bardo was looking past her toward the dining area and the four men.

"I just had a few more questions for you and Mr. Taylor about the case," he said. "Is Mr. Taylor here?"

Jason walked to the door. "Lieutenant Bardo, good to see you," he said.

"Mr. Taylor?" said Bardo. "Am I interrupting something?"

"Not at all. Come in, lieutenant." Jason walked Bardo into the dining area. "These are four friends of mine, Tommy,

Hector, Joe and Andru. Guys, this is Broward County Detective Lieutenant Grady Bardo. He's working on the shootings case."

Tommy walked over to Bardo and extended his hand. "Tommy Ziker, lieutenant. It's a pleasure to meet one of Broward County's finest. I suppose this looks a bit odd. Let me explain. I own the Ziker Detective Agency in Boca Raton. Jason and I served together for five years in the Rangers. I talked him into moonlighting with us tonight on a case up in Palm Beach County where we have to be undercover."

Bardo looked at Andru and all his supplies. "I've got to hand it to you, Mr. Ziker, when you go undercover you don't mess around. It looks like you could give our guys some tips."

"Actually, lieutenant," said Jason, "I thought I would impress these guys and get Andru here, our theater department makeup director, to come over and show us what he could do. What do you think?"

"If I didn't know who you are, I wouldn't recognize you," said Bardo, peering closely at Jason's face.

Di had gone silent. She wanted to see how they would get out of this.

"You said you had some additional questions," said Jason.

"Right," said Bardo, still staring. "When I questioned Rico Valbuena over the weekend, he made reference to a photo he thought I had seen. The way he said it I got the feeling it was an incriminating photo. When I attempted to ask him more about it, he clammed up and said there really was no photo.

Would you or Ms. Herrera have any idea what photo he was referring to?"

Di looked at Jason. Bardo noted that it was the same way that Tomas had looked at Reina when he asked them the same question.

Di spoke first. "The only photos I can think of, lieutenant, are the lineup photos you showed my parents."

"Did you search the photos on Victor's phone?" asked Jason. "what about when Miami-Dade searched Victor and Rico's units? Did you look through what they found?"

"Yes, I did. Nothing that would warrant the importance that Rico seemed to put on it."

Bardo was at the table, looking at the face prosthetics that Andru had laid out. "Do you mind if I pick up one of these?" he asked Andru.

"Be my guest," said Andru. Andru was being very cool, thought Jason ... all things considered.

"I should put our undercover disguise officer in touch with you. She could learn something."

Andru took out one of his cards and handed it to Bardo. "I would be honored to assist law enforcement," he said. "Tell her to contact me anytime."

"Do you mind if I ask what kind of case you're working on?" Bardo asked Tommy.

"Human trafficking," said Tommy. "Parents hire us to help find their runaway children. More times than not, traffickers have snatched them up. There's a bar they hang out at up in Pompano. We're going to go there, pose as buyers and see if we can get a lead on some of these kids."

"I wish you well," Bardo said to him. He turned to Jason and Di. "That about covers it. Sorry about barging in on you. Good luck on *your* case."

Di walked him to the door. On the way back to his unmarked car, Bardo's bullshit detector was going off and had hit the red zone. He got in, drove down the street, away from Jason's condo, like he was leaving the community. At Palm Ave., he took a left, went down to the next street, took another left, back into Jason's community, circled back to Jason's street, parked about a half block from his condo and waited.

Back in the condo Jason asked Tommy if he thought Bardo had bought their story.

"Hard to say," said Tommy. "His prey is Rebecca Cross, not us. It wouldn't surprise me, though, if he hangs around and follows us when we leave."

Andru was back at work on Hector and Joe. "I shouldn't be in trouble, should I?" he asked while fitting a crew cut wig over Hector's shaved head. "He seemed like he liked me. I might even get some extra work with the sheriff's department."

"You're doing great, Andru," said Jason. "You should be fine."

Di was back to looking at Jason from different angles. "God, you look different, Jason. *I* don't even recognize you. You sure had Lieutenant Bardo going."

"We're slightly ahead of schedule," said Tommy. "If it takes thirty or thirty-five minutes to get to Everglades, we should leave at ten-fifteen."

"I'll be leaving a little before ten to go to St. Stephens where the buses are staging," said Di.

By a quarter to ten, Andru was finished working on Joe and Hector and was packing up his materials. "I'm going to leave the adhesive remover here, so you can use it to remove the prosthetics when you're done. I don't suppose I should take a picture for my portfolio."

"Probably not a good idea, Andru," said Jason. "I really appreciate you doing this. Your work is even better than I had imagined."

Tommy, Hector and Joe thanked Andru, and Tommy accompanied him out and retrieved the dark blue windbreakers from his Escalade. He was glad he hadn't brought them in earlier. Seeing them would have surely aroused Bardo's suspicions even more.

Back inside, the four men put on the windbreakers and asked Di what she thought. "I don't see how you guys could look any more official," she told them. Each jacket had "AGENT" in large, white block letters on the back and over the left breast on the front. Tommy, Hector and Joe also had official-looking, but generic, gold detective's badges in their flip-open wallets.

A few minutes later, Di gave Jason a hug – careful not to touch his face, they exchanged air kisses and she left for St. Stephens.

Sitting in his car, Bardo watched Andru leave, saw Tommy retrieve an armful of dark blue something from his vehicle, and saw Di leave a little later. He stayed put. He wasn't interested in them. Fifteen minutes later he watched as the four men came out and got into the Escalade.

Before they left the condo, Tommy told them to take off the jackets and roll them up so they could not be read by anyone who might be observing. Bardo gave them a little time and then pulled out to follow.

∽

Around ten p.m., Carlotta and Maria arrived at Carlos's house. They made small talk for a few minutes before Carlos took the van keys and cash from his pocket and handed them to Carlotta. They decided to leave a little early in case they encountered a traffic delay on their way to Everglades. Carlotta drove.

Neither woman had ever done anything like this before. Maria repeated what she had already told Carlotta more than a few times, "Victor said that they tranquilize these kids before we pick them up."

The panel of plywood was no longer separating the back of the van from the front, since Jason had removed it. Both women had visions of ten desperate immigrant kids overpowering them from behind on the drive back to Allapattah. Carlotta hadn't told Maria, but she had Rico's Smith & Wesson Bodyguard 380 tucked into her waistband.

Cross had told them to arrive at eleven. By the time they got off the freeway at the Andytown exit they had ten minutes to kill, so they pulled into the Shell station there to wait.

The Escalade was within two miles of the Andytown exit when the alert went off on Tommy's phone. "What the hell," he said as he pulled it out and looked at it. "The white van is within two miles of us." He waited for the map to come up on the screen. "It looks like it's parked just off the exit up ahead."

"Maybe there's another pickup scheduled for tonight," said Jason.

"That must be it," said Tommy.

They exited the freeway, turned right and saw the Econoline parked in front of the Shell store.

"I'll bet the pickup is scheduled for eleven, they got here early and are waiting," said Jason.

"Well, we're not waiting," said Tommy, driving past.

With the light, nighttime traffic, Lt. Bardo had no trouble following the Escalade at a distance that prevented him from being spotted. As he passed the Shell station he did not notice the white van parked in front. After he turned onto the frontage road he stopped and waited until the Escalade had turned left onto the dark road that led to Everglades. He slowly drove to the road, turned off his headlights, turned left and followed. The night was totally overcast and Bardo couldn't see a thing, except the brightly-lit facility about a quarter mile down the road.

He lowered his right back window and shone his narrow-beam flashlight at the roadside behind him. He didn't want the light to be observed from the facility and as soon as he detected a flat opening, he planned to back his car into it and off the road. He soon spotted an open area and backed his car in and as far off the road as possible while still being able to observe the front entrance.

The four buses were already assembled at St. Stephens when Di arrived at ten-fifteen. She parked her Prius at a far edge of their lot so as to leave room for the forty or so volunteer vehicles that would soon be arriving.

Father Pat saw her get out of her car and waved her over to the group of drivers and translators/counselors who would be riding along. Reina would be on the second bus. When all were assembled, Father Pat asked everyone to bow their heads and he said a prayer: "Heavenly Father, please bless and watch over our wonderful volunteers tonight, as well as your children who we hope to deliver from inhumane conditions and reunite with their families. Amen." All repeated, "Amen," and went back to talking amongst themselves. The buses were scheduled to depart for Everglades at ten-forty.

CHAPTER 44

U sing his binoculars, Bardo watched as the Escalade pulled up to the front entrance to the Everglades facility and Jason, Tommy, Hector and Joe got out, all wearing blue jackets with AGENT on the back. The lieutenant doubted that Cross or any of the staff would have seen these men before, so they must be wearing the disguises so that they cannot later be identified on the surveillance videos. What the hell are they up to, he wondered.

Inside Everglades, Officer Williams, the only African-American guard at Everglades, was controlling the front door from his seat behind a counter about twenty feet back from the entrance. The men had agreed that Tommy would take the lead on getting in and, once inside, Jason would show the photo to Cross and secure her cooperation.

Williams had watched with curiosity as they pulled up, got out and approached the glass door. Once they reached it, Tommy took out his wallet, held his badge up to the glass and pointed to the door handle.

Rebecca Cross had also been watching the men pull up and walk to the door from her office. She assumed this was the DCA inspection team that Tyler McReedy had told her was coming.

Williams knew nothing about the inspection team, didn't know who these men were, and hesitated buzzing them in.

Cross had gotten up and was walking out of her office to greet the team. She could tell that Williams had not buzzed them in yet.

"Williams," she yelled, "what are you waiting for? Let those men in!"

The buzzer sounded and the four men entered Everglades. They had agreed that they would use names of their sports heroes as their agent names. Thus, Cross was soon introducing herself to Agents Rivera, DiMaggio, Marino and James. They were wondering why she was acting as if she expected them. Once the introductions were done, Jason took Cross aside, took out his phone and showed her the photo. Her jaw almost hit the floor. She didn't know what to think. How could DCA possibly have this photo? She wasn't able to think about it for long.

"There are a lot of people who would be very interested to see this photo and hear the story behind it," Jason said to Cross, who had a totally uncomprehending look on her face. "But," he continued, "this is your lucky week because we haven't shown it to any law enforcement yet. And we never will, as long as you cooperate. Do you understand?"

"Hell no, I don't understand." She lowered her voice, "What do you want?"

"I want you to inform all of your staff that DCA is transferring all of the children to facilities elsewhere. Right now. The first bus should be pulling up in …" he looked at his watch, "four minutes."

"How do I know you won't show that picture to the law?"

"I guess you'll just have to take our word for it." Rebecca looked like she was frozen in place. "Well?" asked Jason.

Rebecca walked over to the counter that Williams was sitting behind. "Officer Williams," she said, "hand me the microphone and set the transmit to facility-wide." Williams did as she ordered. "Attention all staff," she said into the mic, "a DCA team has just arrived and informed me that all of our detainees are to be transferred out of our facility tonight … beginning now. Buses will be pulling up to the front entrance shortly. Please begin an orderly exiting of all detainees immediately."

Lt. Bardo was still waiting in his car, in the darkness, wondering what could be going on inside. He had no jurisdiction at this federal facility, so he couldn't just go walk up to the door and flash his badge and demand entrance. The irony of this thought occurred to him almost immediately. He looked at his watch and saw that it was two minutes to eleven. Just then, the white van passed him. The white van might as well be the white whale … he had been searching for it since this case began. What could they have to do with Jason and the other men in the Escalade? All he could do was watch and wait. If that van picked up kids, he would call for backup and pull it over as soon as it left DCA property.

Carlotta backed the van up and parked next to the Escalade, as close to the front door as she could get. Inside, Joe had seen her pull up and was poking Tommy and Hector to look out front. Carlotta got out and walked up to the front door. She wasn't sure how this worked. Was she supposed to come inside? Or do they bring the kids out to her. Then she saw the four men in the agent jackets

Rebecca Cross was on her walkie talkie barking out instructions to individual guards. She noticed the others were looking at the front door. She turned around and saw Carlotta at the door and the white van behind her with its back doors open. Their eyes met. Cross shook her head. Carlotta cursed, closed the van doors, got back in and pulled away.

Bardo was watching the white van leave the parking lot and come back toward him at about the same time he heard the unmistakable hiss of a large vehicle's pneumatic air brakes. He turned to his left just in time to see a full-size charter bus turn off the frontage road and head toward him. The bus and the van passed each other right in front of his position. He didn't have to think twice about it – he was going after the van.

As soon as the bus passed, he fell in behind the van with his headlights still off. He radioed to dispatch that he was following a white Econoline van and would be pulling it over under the I-75 overpass at exit 23. The occupants were suspects in three attempted code five's in district two. License number to follow. He requested two backup units.

As soon as he turned onto the frontage road, Bardo turned on his headlights and got close enough to the van to call in the license number. When Carlotta turned left toward the underpass, Bardo turned on the flashing blue and red light bar mounted in his grill.

Maria was fairly calm about being pulled over. "They've got nothing on us," she told Carlotta. "We're just out for a drive." She didn't know about the gun in Carlotta's waistband.

Carlotta's heart started racing as soon as she saw the flashing lights. She had already taken the Smith & Wesson from her waistband while pulling over and was now frantically trying to wipe her finger prints from it using her shirt. Once she wiped it down, she planned to hide it under her seat and later claim she knew nothing about it being there.

She had put the van in park and had it almost all wiped down when the explosion of a gunshot filled the van. The 380 had gone off and hit Maria in the side. Carlotta dropped the gun on the floor and both women were screaming. Carlotta opened her door and screamed, "Help, she's been hit!"

Lt. Bardo had exited his car and was crouched behind his open door with his gun trained on the driver's door.

"Driver, put both your hands outside," he shouted.

Carlotta's hands soon appeared. "It was an accident," she yelled. "We need help."

"Keep your hands where I can see them and get out of the vehicle," he ordered.

He could see that she was doing as she was told. "Lay down on the ground, face down, with your hands outstretched."

As Carlotta was doing as ordered she continued yelling, "My friend has been shot. She needs help. It was an accident."

The first Broward County backup cruiser had arrived and parked behind Bardo's car. That deputy assumed a ready-to-fire position behind his opened door.

"My friend has been shot. She can't get out. Call an ambulance," Carlotta screamed from her prone position.

"Where is the gun?" yelled Bardo.

"I dropped it in the van."

"Who's in the back of the van?"

"No one. It's just us two. Somebody help Maria."

Bardo stood and slowly approached Carlotta with his gun trained on her. As he got to the open driver's door, he took a split-second peek inside. Maria was slumped against the passenger door, holding her side which was bleeding profusely. He took a better look inside and saw the gun laying on the floor on the driver's side.

"Call for an ambulance," he yelled back to the deputy before cuffing Carlotta behind her back.

A second Broward County Deputy arrived and, after Bardo had determined that Maria did not have a weapon, began blocking off the road in both directions with cones from his trunk.

The first charter bus had now pulled up to the front entrance to Everglades and opened its door. Di and Father Pat stayed inside the bus so as not to arouse suspicion that this was not a real DCA transfer pickup. Inside, Tommy, Hector and Joe were talking and joking with the guards like they were colleagues. Jason was standing off to the side with an impassive Rebecca Cross.

The first of the children were led to the front door, where Tommy stepped in and took over leading them outside to the bus. Some clutched a stuffed animal or a jacket … their only remaining possessions. Many were whispering to each other their surprise that they hadn't been handcuffed.

Once the first of them boarded the bus, Father Pat began greeting them in Spanish: "Hello, I am Father Sullivan. You are now in the care of Catholic Charities. You have nothing to fear." The children were orderly and Di kept them moving so the bus could be filled as quickly as possible.

Ten of the children in the first group were those that Rebecca had selected to be sold to Carlotta and Maria. They were noticeably drowsy and shuffled along with vacant stares. Once they were on the bus, Di recognized Antonio.

"Antonio," she exclaimed, as he made his way down the aisle toward her. "We've found Isabella," she told him in Spanish, as he reached her. The news snapped him out of the haze he was in.

"Yes? Yes? Where is Isabella? Is she alright?"

"Yes, she's alright. She is in a facility in Texas. You will be staying with a family, or in a church, here in Florida. Lawyers will try and get permission from the government for both of you to go to your aunt's in Houston." Di motioned for Antonio to sit down in the closest seat. She took a notebook and pen from her pocket and sat down next to him. "I need to write down your aunt's name and any contact information you have for her."

"Rosa Flores," Antonio told her. He had memorized her phone number and the town she lived in - Katy, Texas - before leaving San Pedro Sula. Di wrote down the information and made a mental note to be sure to later get the phone number of where Antonio would be staying. She got up, touched his cheek, and went back to seating the children.

The other three buses had arrived and were lined up behind the first bus. Each had its own bi-lingual priest as the on-board greeter. The buses were driven by parishioner volunteers who held Class B commercial drivers licenses with passenger endorsements, a Florida requirement for driving this size passenger bus.

By now, dozens more children were lined up and waiting for the first bus to pull out and the second to pull up. As each of the buses loaded, they pulled out onto the road and waited until all were loaded and ready to go.

As the last of the children followed each other out of the building Jason turned to Cross, "Is that all of them?"

"Officer Williams, is that all of the detainees?" she called over to the guard … her voice actually cracked.

"That's all of them, chief," he answered.

Chief Cross stood staring at Jason. She didn't know if these guys were DCA, DHS or someone else and didn't really care, as long as they left and she could stay free until her plane left the next day.

"Chief Cross," said Jason, "we appreciate your cooperation. You kept your part of the bargain and we'll keep ours." He walked over to join Hector and Joe, the three of them walked outside to where Tommy was waving off the last bus. The four men got into the Escalade and followed.

CHAPTER 45

When the first bus got to where they should turn left to go under the overpass and get on the freeway going east, the driver saw that the road was closed by the police. He asked Father Pat what to do now.

"Let's get on I-75 going west. The next exit where we can turn around is down about twelve miles at the Broward County Rest Area. I'll call the other buses and let them know what we're doing."

Tommy, Jason and the Escalade were behind the last bus. When they got to the intersection, they saw the white van, police cars and ambulance under the freeway.

"I told you Bardo would follow us," said Tommy.

"Looks like the buses are going down to the next exit so they can turn around and head back," said Jason.

Tommy pulled the Escalade off on the shoulder of the entrance ramp. "Switch places with me, Jason," he said. "I have to get on my phone and de-program the tracking device."

Once the police towed the van in and searched it, they would certainly find the tracking device and, unless the data on it was erased, the police would know about the involvement of all of them. Hector had wiped it clean of fingerprints as he was installing it. Now all of their addresses and phone numbers needed to be wiped from its memory.

∽

Carlotta was still laying face down on the pavement as Lt. Bardo stepped over her and got into the van's driver's seat to talk to Maria. Maria was leaning back in her seat and against the passenger door and holding both hands to the bullet wound in her left side.

"The ambulance is on it's way, Maria," said Bardo. "How are you doing?"

"How do you *think* I'm doing? I've been shot. It hurts like hell."

Bardo took out his phone, held it up so he could see it, and turned it on to record. "Maria," he said to the gang banger, "This is not going to get any better until you tell me the truth about Rebecca Cross."

Maria turned and looked at him. He could see she was in terrible pain. "That bitch is bad news," she said. In her mind, she now blamed Cross for everything. "Yeah, she was selling kids. She sold them to Victor and she was going to sell more to us. She waved us off, though, after we got there. We were going back home. And that shit about Miguel wanting a job was bullshit, too."

Bardo turned his head as the deputies were lifting Carlotta to her feet and saw the ambulance coming down the exit ramp. He needed to move his vehicle before he was completely blocked in by the growing number of response vehicles.

"Thank you, Maria," he said as he was getting out. "Here comes the ambulance. Hang in there." He then told the first deputy to get a statement from Carlotta, then take her in and book her on whatever applies. He had another arrest to make.

Bardo pulled his car out just as the ambulance was arriving. He knew, from the background he had done on her, that Cross drove a white, late-model F-150. He hoped she hadn't left Everglades and slipped by while he was occupied with the two women. This time, he drove all the way *to* Everglades, saw a white F-150 still in the lot, and drove back to his previous spot to wait.

Captain Tony Lopez had been sitting in his cubicle working on a crossword when Jason and the fake agents arrived. He stood to see what was going on when he heard Cross call to Williams to open the front door. He wasn't sure who these guys were, but he figured they weren't bringing good news as far as he was concerned. While Cross and Williams were occupied with the visitors, Lopez slipped out the control room's rear door and into the hallway, walked to the far back door, left the building, walked around the outside of the fence perimeter to the front parking lot, got into his vehicle and was pulling out as the first bus was pulling in. He hadn't seen the white Econoline arrive and then leave, but he slowed and watched from a distance as a black car followed and then pulled over the departing van. Tony did the same as the buses would and got on the freeway headed west to the first opportunity to turn around.

After the children and agents had left, Cross told her staff to continue with their shifts as normal. There was still fifteen minutes until her shift ended at midnight. Cross wanted to leave early and had called Captain Lopez on her walkie talkie to leave him in charge, but got no response. She had no time or desire to hunt him down and simply told Officer Williams she would see him tomorrow as she left.

She still wasn't quite sure what had just happened with the agents and the transfers, but was relieved to realize that she didn't care. As she got into her truck and started it up, she could almost see the beaches and swaying palm trees of Micronesia. Her new plan was to load her bags into her truck as soon as she got home and head straight for Miami International. In her growing panic, she no longer cared about selling her vehicle. She would simply leave it in long-term parking and wait in the airport for her flight to depart.

She was so focused on her escape and her future life, she didn't notice Bardo's car backed into the brush off the road as she passed. Once she got to the stop sign at the end of the road, though, she glanced into her rearview mirror and wondered, "where the hell did that car come from". It followed her as she turned right and then the flashing red and blue light bar came on. She pulled over, hoping it was maybe just a rolling stop violation. Once stopped, she could see in her mirror that it was an unmarked car behind her, not a county deputy's patrol car.

Bardo sat in his car informing dispatch that he had just pulled over a suspect in his attempted murder investigation, and included Cross's name, vehicle description and license number. As soon as he got out of his car, Cross saw in her driver's door mirror that it was Bardo.

The visions of beaches and palm trees were gone in an instant ... replaced by the blackness of pure panic. Cross shifted into drive and floored the F-150. She saw the same police roadblock around the white van under the overpass that the others had seen and sped straight up the same freeway entrance headed west.

Bardo was in hot pursuit and radioing for backup to fall in behind him. Cross was doing ninety and still accelerating when she reached the freeway. She wanted to do a u-turn and cross the depressed, grassy median and head back east as soon as the guard cables bordering the inside shoulder ended. Finally, after a half-mile they ended. She braked hard, jerked the wheel left and was speeding through the grass down into the depression, expecting to fly back up the other side and onto the eastbound lanes.

What had looked like a firm grass median in the freeway lights was actually, in the center, a grass-topped bog. Her truck was violently stopped as soon as it hit the muck. After bouncing off the steering wheel, Cross grabbed her purse and jumped out of the truck to run. Instead, she immediately was mired up to her ankles and went sprawling on her face as she tried to take her first step.

Bardo knew what lay in the median, had stopped his car on the firm grass just off the inside shoulder and had a fine view of the finale to her escape attempt. She had only been able to get back up to her knees in the muck. Once he reached her and confirmed she wasn't armed, he cuffed her behind her back.

Two deputies had arrived and were hurrying down the slope to them. When they reached the truck, Bardo instructed them to help get her to her feet. He reached into her pickup and turned off the lights and the engine, then picked up her purse from the mud where she had fallen.

Finally, they were face-to-face. Cross, - spitting grass and algae, the front of her uniform soaking wet - was glaring at Bardo. The detective calmly read her rights to her, informing her that she was under arrest for the attempted murders of Robin and John Herrera and Jason Taylor. He would contact the FBI about the human trafficking once he was back at his district office in Dania Beach.

As the four of them walked back up the grassy slope, Bardo told the deputies that he would be taking the prisoner in himself and they were to stay and process the scene and wait for the truck to be towed out.

Bardo noticed that it was still hot and humid out and that he was sweating as he reluctantly put his hand to the top of

Cross's head and loaded her into his back seat. It had been a long day and night and he had no desire to talk during the drive to the Pompano Beach booking station for females. There would be plenty of time to question Cross tomorrow. On the drive to booking he dispatched a team to pick up Tony Lopez at his home.

Rebecca Cross had no desire to talk, either. She displayed the body language of a large woman whose dreams have just been shattered. She felt like she should be thinking and planning, but she couldn't … she was too numb.

CHAPTER 46

The volunteers who were assembled in St. Stephens' parking lot had been informed that the buses would arrive twenty to thirty minutes late due to the detour. Since they had extra time, St. Stephens' assistant pastor had the volunteers re-park their cars in four equal groups, with room between them for the buses to pull in. They all agreed that the assigning of which children go with which volunteers, and the documenting of all of it needed to be started and finished as quickly as possible.

Parish volunteers were ready with clipboards and printed sheets listing the names of all of the shelter volunteers, with enough space next to each name to record the name and origin of the children leaving with them. Additional information, such as the names of their family members with whom they came to the U.S., would be collected later.

The buses finally arrived at twelve-twenty. On the way, Father Pat and the other onboard priests had explained to the children what was happening and that they would soon be matched up with volunteers who would house them while Reina's organization worked to locate their family members and the ACLU worked to reunite them. The children would still be subject to America's immigration laws, but the goal was to reunite them with their family members, even if the result was family detention in one of the Texas camps while awaiting their court decisions.

The next morning, Catholic Charities and the ACLU would arrange a conference call with the appropriate Homeland Security officials. They would explain to DHS what had occurred and why, citing the trafficking and other abuses at Everglades, and stressing that they stood ready to work *with* DHS to assist reuniting the families involved.

∽

After they arrived back at Jason's condo the four men took turns using the adhesive remover to get Andru's prosthetics off their faces before washing off the glue remnants in Jason's bathroom. It was one a.m. before Tommy, Hector and Joe left.

Jason settled into his easy chair, closed his eyes and waited for Di. That's where she found him, snoring, after she let herself in a half-hour later.

She walked over to him, bent down and whispered in his ear, "We did it."

Jason's eyes opened and he reached up and eased her onto his lap where she lay her head against his chest as he stroked her hair. They sat like that in silence for a few moments, reflecting.

Finally, Jason said, "I'm going to visit Bardo in the morning, give him a copy of the photo and tell him what we know."

"I'm glad," said Di, "I was feeling guilty holding that back from him while he was working so hard on my parents' case." She stood up and continued, "I'm going to stay up and finish my story. I'm still wide awake and want to send it to the Herald as soon as possible."

"I'm impressed with your work ethic," said Jason, getting up. "Your editor and agent is going to bed."

"Oh! I have to call my dad and tell him everything went okay," Di remembered out loud. "He was really worried."

Jason moved to kiss Di goodnight. "Wait a minute," she said. "You can't go to bed yet. You have to tell me what happened with you guys and Chief Cross at Everglades. It'll just take me a minute to call my dad. Don't go anywhere."

Officer Ayesha Bradley, a short, wide and upbeat African-American woman in her mid-thirties, was in charge of booking and processing on the midnight-to-eight shift at Broward County's Pompano Beach Booking Facility. She looked up from her computer when she heard Bardo enter her area with the still-handcuffed Chief Cross who looked mad enough to chew tacks and spit them at you.

"What do we have here, detective?" she asked, once she saw the chief. "You pull her out of a swamp?"

"That's pretty close to the truth, Bradley," said Bardo, who removed Cross's cuffs and then handed her some paper towels from the fingerprint station to wipe the remaining algae and grass off her face and arms. The front of the Chief's brown uniform shirt and long pants were still obviously wet.

As Bradley led Chief Cross to the mugshot station, she turned back to Bardo and said, "This one's going viral, I know it."

Cross, feeling superior even though she was the one being booked, fought the urge to talk back. She was recalling the years when she had been the one leading lowlife prisoners through this same drill at the Panhandle Detention Center.

"What is she, some kind of rent-a-cop?" Bradley asked Bardo as she took the mugshots.

"Something like that," he answered, before leaving to start writing his report. He would get the essentials down now, go home and get a few hours sleep, then finish the rest of it at his Dania Beach office in the morning. Tomorrow would be another full day.

CHAPTER 47

———

When Lt. Bardo arrived at work on Wednesday morning at the Dania Beach District Office, the front desk officer told him he had a visitor sitting in the waiting area. He looked over and saw Jason Taylor stand and walk toward him.

"Mr. Taylor, you're looking more like yourself this morning."

The two men shook hands.

"Good morning, lieutenant. Is there somewhere private where we can talk?"

"There aren't too many private places in a police station. Will my cubicle do?"

"That will be fine. I have something to show you."

"Follow me through the maze," said Bardo. "Let me guess … I'll bet it's a photo."

Jason had his phone out and was bringing up the picture of the van from Thursday night. They sat down at Bardo's desk and Jason handed him the phone.

Bardo studied it, recognized Victor and Miguel and said, "So this is the photo everyone has been telling me about. When was it taken?"

"Thursday night. Just outside the Everglades facility."

"You took it?"

"Yes."

"You also subdued these two?"

"That's right."

"But the van ended up back in the hands of the DK's."

"That's a long story."

"Where are the children in the photo now?"

"They're being sheltered by Catholic Charities volunteers while the family members they were separated from are located. Then the ACLU will assign them volunteer immigration lawyers to work on reuniting them."

"That's an honorable task," said Bardo. "As you might imagine, I have a few questions for you. Care for some coffee before we get started?"

"No. Thank you."

Jason explained that he had simply been conducting nighttime surveillance of Everglades after being told of the human trafficking that Tomas had heard rumors of. He left out any mention of Di's involvement, other than her being his source for the information.

"Why didn't you tell me about this right up front, after the shootings?" Bardo asked.

"Because then you would have had to report it the FBI or DHS, and that would have interfered with my plan."

"What was your plan?"

"To get those kids out of that hell hole and to somewhere safe."

"And that's what you and your friends were up to last night?"

"That's right. I think Cross believed we were with her employer, DCA. I showed her the photo I just showed you and told her we were transferring all of the children and if she didn't want us to go to the feds with what we knew, she wouldn't interfere."

"How did you get all the buses? Where were the kids taken?"

"Catholic Charities arranged for the buses and for volunteer families to shelter two to four kids each. They and the ACLU are going to have a conference call with DHS this morning explaining what happened and deciding where to go from here."

"You and your friends took a mighty big risk with all this. Why?"

Jason told Bardo the same thing he had told Tommy Ziker at Patio Joes, finally saying, "We're the good guys, lieutenant. I guess *Rangers Lead the Way* was drilled into me pretty effectively."

"That's all fine," said Bardo, "But it seems to me like the FBI could file a whole range of charges against everyone involved."

"We're hoping that they won't want the government's implication in the human trafficking of children in its care to come out ... which it would if we were charged."

"Isn't that what your friend is writing her story about?"

Bardo asked. He could see that his question had taken Jason by surprise.

"You're right, lieutenant." Jason picked up his phone. "I have to call Di. Do you mind?"

"Go ahead," said Bardo. He wanted to hear this.

Di had been up writing until five and was asleep when her phone rang. "Jason, what's up?"

"Di, I'm here with Lt. Bardo at his office. He just brought up something we hadn't thought of."

"What's that?"

Jason explained to her that not going public with the human trafficking part of the story could be their leverage with the government to avoid getting charged.

"Jason, that's the biggest part of the story," said Di, sitting up in his bed. "What's next, you want me to kill the whole thing?"

Jason expected this wouldn't go over well, and it wasn't. "We should at least hold off until we know how the conference call goes this morning. This could affect all of us, including you, Reina and Father Pat."

"Well, at least let me include the part about you rescuing the kids in the van. Without that we have no tie-in with the gang or my parents' shooting."

"That should be okay," said Jason. "But we should still wait for word about how the conference call went so we know where we stand."

"I've been sitting on this story for a week now. I guess another hour or two won't hurt. Father Pat said he'd phone me as soon as their call was done. I'm going to go take care of my dad. Are you going to work today?"

"No, I took the day off. If you want to email me your story, I can start editing it when I get home."

She told Jason she would and asked him to thank Lt. Bardo again for the work on her parents' case.

After ending the call, Jason gave Bardo Di's message and then asked him, "So, what happened with the white van last night? I saw you had it pulled over under the freeway."

Bardo told him it looked like Victor's girlfriend and Rico's wife were supposed to pick up more kids from Cross, but they had seen Jason and his friends inside Everglades and had left.

Bardo had come to like and respect this former army ranger. Although he was careful not to reveal anything he shouldn't, he almost felt like he was discussing the case with a colleague. He went on to describe to Jason how Carlotta had accidentally shot Maria as he was pulling them over, and that Maria had confirmed to him Cross's involvement in the trafficking and the shootings.

"Were you able to arrest Cross, then?" Jason asked.

"I waited until she left work and was off DCA property. I tried to pull her over but she ran, going west on seventy-five. She tried to do a u-turn through the median, got bogged down in the middle, got out and tried to run and fell on her face."

"Did *you* get a picture?"

The lieutenant laughed, "No, I should have. She was a sight." Bardo started organizing papers on his desk. "Anyway, we should be able to nail her as an accomplice in the shooting of the Herreras and the attempt on you." He stood, "Right now I have to get with the FBI about the trafficking."

"Give me your email address and I'll send you the photo of the van," said Jason. "How do you think they'll react to my involvement?"

"As far as I'm concerned, you did the right thing, and that's what I'll tell them. It won't hurt if you can get the ACLU and DHS to back your play, too." Bardo held out his hand, "Thanks for coming in today, Jason, I appreciate it. I'll keep you and the Herreras informed."

"You have my number if you need me to answer any more questions."

CHAPTER 48

———⁓———

W hen Di arrived home, she passed by the kitchen on her way to see her dad in his bedroom. Heather was fixing breakfast.

"Diamond," called out Heather as she stirred scrambled eggs, "It's so nice of you to stop by. I suppose you needed to pick up another outfit."

Di walked into the kitchen and kissed Heather on the cheek. "It's so nice to see you, too, Aunt Heather." She leaned over the frying pan, "Mmm, smells good. We're so lucky to have you here." She turned and walked to the bedroom.

John sat up straight when he saw her walk in. "Di! Come here and give me a hug. You made it." Di went over and hugged her dad. "You're not out on bail or anything, are you?" he asked, half joking.

"No. Everything went exactly as planned. Jason and the others got all the kids out and they're now all being sheltered by volunteer families."

"I know you," he said. "I can tell when something's bothering you. Is it Heather?"

Di laughed and looked to make sure her aunt wasn't about to walk in. "No, it's not Heather." Di sat down in a chair next to the bed. "I have to hold off on submitting my story until

we know how the conference call went with Homeland Security."

"Why is that?"

"We may have to make a deal with the feds: we won't go
public about human trafficking at Everglades and, in return,
they won't charge any of us for moving the children."

Just then, Heather walked in with John's breakfast and set
it on his bed table. "I'm sorry, but I didn't make enough for
you, Di. I had no idea you would be here. John, do you need
anything else? If not, I'm going down to sit with Robin." She
kissed John on the cheek, told him she would see him around
dinner time and left the room, without another word to Di.

Once she was gone, Di asked her dad, "Is it just me, or is
she a real bitch?"

John had just taken a bite of his scrambled eggs, but that
didn't keep him from laughing. "No, it's not just you, but I
can't say a harsh word while I'm eating her breakfast."

Di's phone rang. She looked and saw it was Father Pat.
"Excuse me, dad, I have to take this. Father Pat, hi, tell me
how it went."

The priest told her that basically, the two DHS officials
they spoke with were shocked ... shocked by the human trafficking and shocked by the midnight transfer of all of the
immigrant children. They understood the reasoning and mo-
tivations of Catholic Charities, the ACLU and the volunteers.

"Are they going to charge any of us?"

"They told us at this time they have no plans for that,
providing that all of the children have been documented and

are accounted for. They actually almost sounded grateful that we had uncovered and stopped this. Or, I should say *you* uncovered and stopped this. Those kids are all in your debt, Diamond. If you hadn't pursued your story, none of this would have happened."

"Father, I think I'm blushing. You're too kind. But, speaking of my story, did the DHS people indicate any opposition to the human trafficking aspect being made public in the press?"

"No. In fact, it sounded like they were eager to see Chief Cross and anyone who helped her prosecuted to the full extent of the law. I think they want to make an example of her to the other private detention contractors. You might want to interview them yourself."

Before hanging up, Father Pat gave Di the names and contact information for the two DHS officials who were on the conference call.

After hanging up she turned to John. "Dad, that was great news. DHS *wants* the trafficking publicized. In fact, Father Pat suggested I interview them, too."

"Now you look like my girl again. You were really worried, weren't you?"

"Damn right I was worried. This is my story and I want to get it all out there. I feel like I'm hyperventilating. I need to get your dressing changed, then I need to call Jason, then I need to call these DHS guys. I brought my laptop so I can work in my room." She leaned in and gave her dad another hug, careful not to knock over his breakfast. "I love you, dad.

Keep eating. I'll be right back with a fresh bandage."

"As soon as you're done, I'm going to call your mother with the news. Oh, I almost forgot to tell you, her doctors said she can probably come home on Friday."

Once in her room, Di called Jason, gave him the good news, and then emailed him her story file so he could start editing. She was able to reach one of the DHS officials who had been on the conference call, Sarah Takashi, the director of immigrant detention facilities for the southeast U.S.

Ms. Takashi confirmed that her department stood ready to work with Catholic Charities and the ACLU on the family reunifications of the children from Everglades. For most, this would just mean that they would be detained elsewhere until their cases were decided, but at least they would be with their family members. She also confirmed that DHS had no problem with Di exposing the trafficking and other abuse at Everglades in her article.

During their time on the bus the night before, Di had spoken extensively with Antonio and much of what he told her would be featured in her story. She added a couple of new paragraphs, cleaned up a few others and emailed Jason the updated file. She was anxious to get back to the condo, wrap up the story, submit it and then celebrate. She texted Jason that she should be there in about an hour and suggested they invite Reina and Tomas over to celebrate with them later. Then she gathered up her things and went into the kitchen to fix John some lunch and put it in the fridge for him. He had recently started walking again, with the aid of a cane.

CHAPTER 49

B y a little after one, Di and Jason were standing at his breakfast bar poring over the final edit of her story on her laptop.

"I think you nailed it, Di. What do you think?"

"I don't know. I've never written anything this complex, or important, before. I think it's ready, though. Let's do it."

Di already had the intro email composed to Bert Friedman at the Herald. She attached the story file and the van photo, put the curser on *send* and they both put their fingers on the *enter* button and pushed it simultaneously.

Jason insisted on a high-five and then they hugged, with Di saying, "All of a sudden, I'm nervous as hell."

They parted and Jason said, "I think that's perfectly normal." He walked to the refrigerator and came back with a bottle of Veuve Clicquot Brut champagne that he had picked up on his way back from seeing Bardo. "But I have just the thing for young journalist nerves."

He set up and filled two champagne glasses that he had pre-positioned out of Di's view.

Jason lifted his glass to her and said, "Here's to the bravest, smartest, most beautiful woman I have ever known."

They both sipped their champagne, looking at each other.

Di had tears welling up in her eyes. "I hope you didn't get that from your wine guy, too."

Jason took her glass and put them both on the bar and took her in his arms again and kissed her. Still holding her he said, "I think our first week went pretty well. What do you say we try a second?"

All of a sudden, Di heard a song playing in her head that she didn't even know she knew, *Baby, I'm Yours.* Well, she thought, the subconscious doesn't lie.

They parted and Di reached over to her purse, took out a tissue and started dabbing her eyes. "I know I don't look like it, but I'm really happy right now."

Just then, the ring tone started on Di's phone. She picked it up and looked at the screen. "It's the Herald!" she cried. "Hello, this is Di Herrera."

It was Bert Friedman. Di put her phone on speaker.

"Mr. Friedman, this is a big surprise. Jason Taylor is here, too. I have you on speaker."

"Hello Jason. I want to thank you for sending Ms. Herrera our way with her story."

"Hey Bert. What do you think?"

"Well, I think I'm looking at tomorrow morning's lead story."

Jason and Di were making shocked and amazed happy faces at each other.

"I just wanted to clarify a couple of things before I send it on."

The clarifications that Friedman wanted were minor and

they were done after a few minutes. Before ending the call, Friedman added, "Ms. Herrera, prepare yourself. I would say that by dinnertime, your story will have been picked up by the wires, then by the online news feeds like Google and Yahoo. I wouldn't be surprised if you get late-night calls from cable and network news producers."

"You're kidding, right?" Di responded.

"I'm not kidding. Buckle up."

"Bert," interjected Jason. "Getting back to basics, I'm Di's agent. How much is the Herald paying for her story?"

"Well, I'm going to go way beyond what I would normally pay a rookie, but less than I would have to pay a veteran … five thousand. Ms. Herrera, accounting will get with you about whatever forms and numbers we'll need. I've gotta go. Thanks again."

"Wow," said Di to Jason. "Did you ever get ahold of Reina to see if she and Tomas were coming over? I need to get grounded."

"Lead story. Miami Herald," said Jason, staring at her. "Yeah, she said they'd come by around three."

"Let's bring the champagne and go sit down," said Di, and they were soon on the couch. "Did he say TV news?"

"That's what he said." Jason took another sip of his champagne.

"I have to do something with my hair."

Jason picked up her glass and handed it to her. "Relax, Di. Let it come to you. Besides," he said, smiling, "they *have* hair people."

"You're right," she said, taking a sip. "Of course they have hair people."

Jason put his glass down, saying, "I'm going to go get some snacks. I'll be right back."

Di grabbed his arm before he could get up, then took his face in both her hands and kissed him. "*You* are incredible," she said, softly. "Thank you … for everything."

Jason squeezed her hand, got up and walked to the kitchen. Just as he got there, Di's phone rang. It was still on the breakfast bar.

She turned and asked, "Jason, can you get that?"

Jason answered her phone, then, "Honey, It's CNN, for you."

THE END